STEAL AWAY

STEAL AWAY

Barrie Wigley

PARTRIDGE

To order additional copies of this book, contact
Toll Free 800 101 2657 (Singapore)
Toll Free 1 800 81 7340 (Malaysia)
orders.singapore@partridgepublishing.com

www.partridgepublishing.com/singapore

ACKNOWLEDGEMENTS

My sincere thanks to Robert Taylor for
the original cover design, and
those who assisted in researching the last
months of WWII. To Que Tong (LLB) for
his legal advice. To the many organisations
who gave advice regarding the research
during the early manuscripts. To my editor
at Apex Reviews and to Mark Jones
(B. Ed. BA.) for proofreading the pre-
edit final. Finally, to Bob and
Louise, Brian and Lisette, for their
support and encouragement
Throughout the writing of this novel.

Barrie Wigley

ONE PERCENT OF SOMETHING IS BETTER THAN
A HUNDRED PERCENT OF NOTHING.

ALSO BY
THE SAME AUTHOR

Sail Away
Get Away
Run Away

CHAPTER 1

ELISE WAS A WORLD CLASS pianist. Although she was starting to show signs of her age, she was still nonetheless a very attractive woman, as well as a first class musician. She had been married to Herman Mies Van Der Rohe for some twenty-seven years.

Herman was a successful banker. He had joined the Goldsworth Commercial Bank after first graduating from the London Kings College, then the Westminster University, where he studied Finance and Languages. Herman was born in England, although his mother was Austrian and his father was Swiss. His parents had come to England soon after the end of the Second World War. Herman's Father, Hedrick, had been offered a position at one of the first Swiss banks to have a branch in London.

Herman had been at the Goldsworth Bank for almost twenty-nine years, having joined after graduating from university with a BA Hons degree. He was now vice-president of the London branch. He was expected to be the next president in about four year's time when the residing president retired. When Elise was away from home,

Herman would often work well into the evening. Elise, when performing at a concert and sometimes in a foreign land, would also be working evenings and the occasional afternoon matinees, as well as regular weekends.

They were a devoted couple, giving everything, first to each other and secondly to their careers. They had no children and never intended to have any. Although they liked children and often donated to the various children's charities, they were happy to leave it that way.

Living in a Tudor manor-house set in three acres of Bedfordshire countryside on the outskirts of Bedford, England, Elise loved her garden. Whenever possible, her relaxation came from looking after the roses in the front and the herb garden just outside the back entrance to the kitchen at the rear of the house. The three-days-a-week gardener would usually look after the rest, pruning the shrubs and trees, tending the lawns and the vegetable plot at the far end of the back garden that overlooked the Bedford Premier golf course. They would both love to spend more time in the garden, but of course it was impossible. Elise liked the idea of a small vegetable garden, if only to have fresh produce with which to cook when she was at home.

Herman was not a member of the golf club and had little interest in playing golf – or any other sport, for that matter—but he and Elise often ate at the restaurant that had a fine reputation. You did not have to be a member of the club to do so; the proprietors were only too happy to greet Herman and Elise to eat at their establishment. On rare occasions, Elise would play the piano in the evening, when not working elsewhere.

Herman had little to do with the running of the house, as he was hardly ever there. Along with the gardener, they had employed Maria more than ten years ago, and she had served them well. Today was no exception.

Maria came in five days a week. Although Herman and Elise had asked her if she would like to move in and occupy one of the several spare bedrooms on a more permanent basis, she had declined, feeling she would lose some, if not all of her independence. It was a decision both Herman and Elise were reluctant but happy to accept.

Today was Wednesday. As usual, Herman had to be at the office early, as it was one of his duties to oversee the unlocking of the bank. Meanwhile, his wife was off playing at a one-night concert in London. Today his work load was light, so it was quite possible he would be able to attend the concert later, after the bank closed; they could return home together afterwards, having an enjoyable dinner together on the way.

Although most of the locks at the bank were on timers and connected to a central security control operation, Herman still needed to be present when the locks automatically opened. He had the necessary codes for the locks in the case of any emergency or other problems, should there be a need to override the timers.

*   *   *

The early morning frost had almost disappeared when Mario Petri climbed the steps to the Goldsworth Bank. In one hand, he was carrying a high quality leather bound black briefcase with gold plated corner trims and front tumbler locks. Under the arm of the same hand, he carried a laptop PC. He approached the outer green glass entrance doors of the Goldsworth Bank with caution; it was his first

3

visit to the bank. It was 10:30 in the morning. He had an appointment to see Herman Mies Van Der Rohe, for the purpose of opening an account using bearer bonds valued at 100,000 GBP he carried in his briefcase.

As a commercial bank, the Goldsworth Bank, whose main headquarters were in Geneva, Switzerland, with branches in Zurich as well as in Austria, dealt only with people who were in commerce or industry. Mario had papers to prove he was in the insurance and investment advisory business, showing he owned the insurance company 'Homes & Autos', of which there were two branches, one in Bedford and one in Northampton.

Mario had chosen the Goldsworth Bank because it was the largest Swiss bank represented in the UK, as well as because of its commercial interests, rather than those of a domestic nature.

The bank had heavy front main doors. Mario took the two steps from the pavement to the outer entrance doors. Inside, he was greeted by a commissionaire, where a brief body search was carried out. Once satisfied, the commissionaire nodded to the security guard behind the second set of bulletproof green tinted glass doors, allowing entry onto the bank's reception floor. Even though this was a commercial bank, security was tight even though the bank carried very little hard currency. The Swiss were fanatical when it came to security, which was why Swiss banking was number one in the world.

Mario proceeded to the counter marked 'Enquiries'.

"I have an appointment to see Mr. Mies Van Der Rohe," he told the lady with a trim figure wearing steel rimmed, brown tinted glasses and gently swept back pepper-grey hair.

"Wait a moment, please," she replied in a soft voice.

A few moments later, Herman appeared at the enquiries desk. Placing his briefcase on the floor between his feet and placing the laptop under his left arm, Mario accepted the outstretched hand.

"A pleasure to meet you, Mr. Petri. Please come with me."

Herman's office was what can only be described as a typical senior banking official's office. There was, for example, a small brass hand bell on his desk; the upper grip was fashioned in the outline of the 'forge' at Gretna Green, north of the border, notorious for 'runaways' to go and get married. There were also pictures in gold frames of previous presidents, and plenty of brass!

Herman had proposed to Elise more than twenty-nine years ago while spending a few days with friends in Scotland and listening to one of her concerts. It had been a packed house and received no less than three curtain calls. It was that very evening Herman made his proposal to Elise. He had only known her a short while. Two years later, they were married.

"I'm told you wish to open an account with us, Mr. Petri," Herman said, extending his hand as an indication for Mario to be seated.

"That's correct," Mario replied. "I have bearer bonds to the value of 100,000 GBP with which to do so, and papers to support my commercial interests."

"Very good, then. Let's get started."

Mario opened his briefcase and handed over the bearer bonds, named so by the fact that whoever was in possession of them at any given time was in fact the owner; no names were attached. In this case, it was now Herman or the bank who owned the bonds—simply by the fact that Mr. Petri had handed the bonds over to the bank official! For a brief moment, Mario was considering walking out. He had worked hard to earn the 100,000 pounds worth of bonds.

Herman typed in a few numbers on his desktop computer keyboard and waited for the screen to come to life. Turning the monitor slightly so Mario could see the screen, he pointed to a row of numbers; this was to be a 'numbered' account, not a named account. Mario in turn typed the number into his laptop and waited briefly for the information to appear on his screen. The new account showed that account number 0416230742 had a credit of 100,000 GBP. Herman pushed a couple of pieces of ready typed paper across to Mario and indicated with a small cross the two places where he was to sign.

Thirty minutes later, Mario let out a sigh of relief. Back out on the street, he raised his hand to block out the glare of the sun; it had been quite dark in Herman's office. Although it was early November, it was a bright day for the time of the year, and the sun was shining low on the horizon. Mario paused to let his eyes adjust to the daylight. He was now ready to put the second part of his plan into operation.

*   *   *

Mario returned to his room in Bedford. After taking a shower and changing into something more comfortable, he left in search of some lunch. After lunch, he would drive to Herman's house and watch until well after the banker returned home. At a little after 11pm, Mario returned home, stopping for a bite to eat at one of the many late night fast food venues on the way. Dawn was breaking when Mario returned to watch the house. He had picked up a fried egg and sausage sandwich on the way from another street vendor.

Mario was keeping a record of the comings and goings of both Elise and Herman. He would be doing this for the next two or three weeks, possibly longer, particularly when Elise was not at home. He needed an accurate account of their comings and goings, and times of when they left or arrived were of the utmost importance; this information was essential if his plan was going to work. He hoped he would be able to work out some consistencies in their comings and goings.

Now well into November, both the mornings and evenings were getting very cold and damp. Mario spent considerable amounts of time in the car with the engine running and the heater on full.

At 9.30pm on the 17th of November, Mario returned home confident that Herman, who had gotten home at 7.30pm, and Elise, who had not left the house all day, would not be going anywhere that evening. This gave Mario the chance to stop at a respectful restaurant and have a decent meal before returning home. Once back home, after two whiskeys on the rocks and a long shower, Mario climbed into bed and was asleep in no time.

CHAPTER 2

O N THE 19TH OF NOVEMBER, a cold, damp, and misty evening, Mario was keeping vigil on Elise and Herman's house. The time was 6.00pm, and Mario decided this was now as good a time as any to put the next part of his plan into operation—depending, of course, on the time of Herman's arrival home from work.

The mist, more a sheet layer of fog, could be to his advantage. Herman arrived at his house at 6.25pm, a little earlier than normal, possibly due to the weather.

Mario had positioned himself near the entrance to the house, and he saw Herman's arrival. To remain incognito, Mario was wearing all black, including a hood and canvas shoes. He used the lawn rather than the gravel driveway to gain the best advantage to position himself.

As Herman climbed the three steps to the front door, Mario slipped in behind him. Under his left arm was a laptop computer. In his right hand, he was carrying a gold plated Walther PPK.

*   *   *

I was sitting in my office going through the day's workload when the phone rang.

After the problems I'd had with the Parkinson affair, Henry, my solicitor of many years and of my parents before me, had suggested I open a P.I. agency. We could well afford to do so with the compensation and other rewards Christina and I had received from the Parkinson estate, not to mention the reward money and settlement from the police compensation unit and a featured article in the 'Northants Post'. He had made the point that with the experience I had gained while working not only with MI5 and MI6, but also with the Northamptonshire constabulary, I was in a good position in that particular area. He felt sure I would do well. With the workload coming in from his various offices, he was sure he could put a considerable amount of work my way—if past experience was anything to go by.

Engineering work was still very thin on the ground, particularly in the Midlands. Companies were taking on 'Agency' personnel when required, rather than having them on their own books full-time, while half the time doing very little.

It seemed I had not disappointed Henry.

I had started with a modest office in Northampton, on a six-month lease. I was now in our new slightly upmarket, second floor office in Bedford, the next county town south of Northampton.

From the outside, it was an ordinary looking building. I was leasing the second storey, with an option to buy. It had windows of tinted green glass, instead of aging plain glass, and internal aluminium doors with similar tinted green glass at the office entrance, rather than the shabby wooden doors at the old office. Some of the furniture was new, and some second-hand, all from respectable sources.

Apart from my advertising in the Yellow Pages and local papers, Henry had put a considerable amount of work my way. On rare occasions, I had been asked to make certain 'discreet' enquiries on behalf of MI5 and MI6 once they found out about my new occupation.

I picked up the phone; it was Henry.

"Brian, I have a small problem. Can you get up to Kaxton later today?"

"I can make it mid-afternoon, if that's okay."

"That's fine, I'll see you then."

I wondered what sort of problem Henry might have that needed my seemingly immediate attention.

*   *   *

Herman felt the prod of something hard in his back; this was most unusual. At first he thought it might be the branch of a shrub, but then there were no shrubs at the entrance to the house.

"Keep moving," a voice muttered from behind.

Herman did as he was told.

Inside, Mario prodded the gun again.

Once inside, he instructed Herman to go through to the dining room, reminding him there was a gun pressed firmly into his back.

Once in the dining room, Mario carefully removed the laptop computer from under his raincoat and placed it on the dining room table, carefully keeping the gun trained on Herman.

From his right-hand pocket he removed a roll of 'gaffer' tape and tossed it over to Herman, with instructions to tape his wife's arms to the back of the chair rest and her legs to the chair legs, as well as place a strip across her mouth so she could not scream.

"Make a hole in the tape covering her mouth," Mario told Herman. This he carefully did with one of the knives from the dining room table Elise had laid ready for dinner.

Once Elise was secured, Mario opened the laptop, carefully keeping Herman within sight. He then plugged the laptop into the nearest socket, entered a few numbers, and pressed enter.

Mario placed the gun back into his raincoat pocket— still keeping it pointed at Herman – then informed them both that the laptop was now an explosive device. In the event of a power failure, the battery had a two hour capacity. Providing Herman did as he was asked, there would be nothing to worry about. They would not be harmed in *any* way.

*   *   *

I travelled the journey to Northampton, then I had to change trains for Caxton. As I left the station, there was a little drizzle in the air; nothing to worry about. It was only a short walk to 'Top Hat Terrace', where Henry had his main Midlands office, a place I had become quite familiar with.

On my arrival, Henry's receptionist informed me that as I was expected, I should go straight to his office, while she would inform him of my arrival.

On reaching Henry's office, the door opened before I could knock.

"Hello, Henry," I said, accepting his outstretched hand. "It's good to see you. How are you these days?"

"Fine, never better, me boy. And you?"

"Likewise," I replied.

"Tea or coffee?" Henry asked.

"My usual, Henry, tea with milk, no sugar, thank you."

Henry had coffee. Once our drinks had been delivered, I asked him what the problem was that needed my attention, seemingly so urgently?

"Well, Brian, it's not so much urgent, but extremely interesting... even intriguing!"

"Do carry on, Henry. I'm listening."

"I'm sure you well remember the Parkinson affair—who could forget?"

"Rightly so," I commented. "Who could forget nine months out of one's life? Down the drain, so to speak. The compensation that was paid, although very helpful, did little to restore my life back the way it was; only my financial position."

"Well, I had a phone call from the accountant at Parkinson's here in Caxton; it seems he is a little concerned that the Parkinson family is using the company for 'laundering money'."

"If I didn't know you better, Henry, I'd say you're kidding me—but I do know you better. What is it you would like me to do about it? You didn't call me up from Bedford just to give me the news. I know you better than that."

*   *   *

Mario guided Herman to the front door, still holding the gun in his pocket; in the other hand was the mobile phone that could activate or neutralize the explosive device in Herman's dining room.

"I repeat, do exactly as I ask, and all will be well. I am very serious."

"Where are we going?" Herman asked in a trembling voice. "Where to...?"

"Your bank, of course."

"Why? It's closed and won't open until 8.30am tomorrow."

"Come, Herman, I have the button right under my left thumb! Remember what I said—if you want your wife to play at another concert."

"Yes, but..."

"No buts. I know you have the codes for the unlocking of the two sets of front doors. I'm not interested in any internal security regarding safety deposit holdings, just access to your office. Now get in the car," Mario prompted Herman.

They drove in silence, the traffic being very light at this time of the evening. The bank was not difficult to find, and Herman knew better than to give Mario wrong directions; he loved his wife too much.

"The bank doesn't carry a lot of money. You see, it's a commercial bank," Herman blurted out.

"I know, Herman. I don't wish to rob your bank. I need you to give my company a loan."

Parking was easy at that time of the evening.

*   *   *

"So what's prompted the Parkinson's chief accountant to contact you?" I asked.

"Well, he remembered I defended you during the earlier Parkinson problem. When I mentioned you'd built up a PI agency, he asked if I might contact you. He suggested maybe we could both meet up."

"I'm happy to go along with that," I ventured.

"I do remember something about Parkinson, the younger brother, diverting some of the profits from the factory he was running; this was to part finance the re-work on his new manor house, which first prompted me to wonder: why does a multimillionaire need to embezzle 'petty cash' to pay towards his personal projects? You will remember, I was the chief engineer of the factory at the time, in title only—of course you would remember. So what is it you're suggesting?" I asked.

"Well, he's a little more than concerned about the whole affair. I'll get in touch with Walter, Walter Prendigast is his name. I'll let him know I've spoken to you about this, and hopefully we can arrange a meeting to discuss the problem."

"Right, Henry. You're the boss. I'll go along with whatever you say."

I got up to leave, accepting Henry's outstretched hand.

"You'll contact me when you have something?"

"I certainly will."

At this point, I left 'Top Hat Terrace' and headed for the train station, the drizzling rain still falling from the sober grey skies. I would get a taxi home from Northampton station and not return to the office today.

CHAPTER 3

MARIO HAD MADE CERTAIN TO emphasise the word 'loan'.

Arriving at the bank, he indicated for Herman to get out of the car and climb the couple of steps to the bank's main entrance doors. He made sure Herman could see his right-hand thumb close to the send button on the mobile phone. They took the three steps up to the bank's main doors, with Mario taking up the rear.

"Now open the doors to the bank, please," Mario instructed Herman. "Remember what's at stake here."

For a single moment, Mario though Herman was going to throw everything away; however, he then entered the codes for the early opening of the two sets of the main front doors.

Once seated in Herman's grand office, Mario passed a slip of paper across to Herman. On the typed paper were the instructions for Herman to make the transfer of four million GB pounds to his recently opened numbered account.

Mario reminded Herman that this *was* to be a loan, and it would be repaid in full—with interest.

Herman set up the loan, then turned the monitor around so Mario could see it had been set up per his instructions.

Mario checked every detail carefully, then took the phone out of his pocket and moved around to Herman's desk. Nudging Herman to stand to one side, he placed the mobile phone on the right of the desk, ensuring a positive distance between the phone and Herman.

Mario then sent a few numbers across the computer screen and pressed enter, thus ensuring Herman could not reverse the authorisation.

Once satisfied the four million plus his original 100,000 GBP had started their journey halfway around the world, Mario patted Herman on the shoulder and repeated yet again that this was only a loan and *would* be repaid.

Mario returned Herman to his house and gave him the phone, with instructions on the correct buttons to press.

Once Mario had departed the scene, he smiled to himself.

There was no bomb!

*   *   *

Fifty years earlier in November 1943, the German *Afrika Korps* was struggling to maintain its presence in North Africa. During late November, General Rommel had a bitter dispute with Hitler over the *Afrika Korps*. The following day, Rommel returned at Hitler's request, whereupon Hitler apologised to him for his raging temper and outbursts. Adolf Hitler was well renowned for his temper and wild outbursts. Later, Hitler told Field Marshal Goering to supply the *Afrika Korps* with whatever Rommel needed. Goering later invited Rommel to accompany him on his private train, along with

Frau Rommel. As the train pulled out of Munich station, Rommel noticed Goering was wearing a rather large emerald studded tiepin, while at the same time displaying a rather large gold and single carat diamond ring on his left hand.

During the journey, Goering made no mention of supplies for the *Afrika Korps*; instead, Goering told of his gathering of statues from North Africa and paintings from Italy, mainly Rome, along with many other artifacts.

Goering spoke of his model railway, the size of a miniature village, and his fascination with trains.

It is reported that Goering gave Rommel the Air Force Pilots Cross, set with diamonds. This, however, was never confirmed.

Goering's only objective was how to get as many paintings from Italy and sculptures from North Africa as he could to fill his train. There was no mention of what the *Afrika Korps* desperately needed—which was the sole purpose of the trip.

* * *

The first of several trains to come pulled out of the sidings at Stuttgart railway station. It was 6:30pm on the 16th of December, 1944. It is nearly a two hundred mile journey to Zurich, and then finally on to Nyon, on the northern shores of Lake Geneva. Due to its unusual cargo, it would take a little longer than normal. Secrecy had been of extreme importance; the fewer who knew of the train's contents, the better.

There would be more trains covering the same trip until all the ill-gotten gains had left Germany, all under the strict supervision of Field Marshal Goering.

It was mid-December; the snow had been falling steadily for well over six hours. With temperatures well below freezing, ice had built up on the tracks.

The man put in charge of the transportation was Colonel Von Hemel Aldrich, an officer who had been personally appointed by Goering himself. He had issued instructions to the driver not to exceed the speed of forty miles per hour at any cost, and he added for the driver to keep a sharp lookout for anything suspicious. With weather conditions as they were, attempts could be made to sabotage the journey; not to sabotage the train for its cargo, but by splint-away groups looking for a way to escape the country.

On board were three tons of German gold. A further two tons were mixed with the melted down assets of the Jews during the Holocaust, such as gold watches and chains, gold teeth, rings and other such items. Four more tons of gold had been plundered from the banks of German-occupied Europe. Three tons of silver were also plundered from countries throughout Europe. Also included were miniature paintings in their original frames, with larger paintings carefully removed from their frames, rolled up, and placed in watertight steel canisters, mostly from France and Italy, a few from inside Germany. Artifacts from Russia, plundered before Russia took back its country, were now carefully packed in medium-sized crates for easy transportation. Lastly, there were small palm-sized sacks of jewelry, again plundered from the Jews, originally intended for use in aiding the German war effort.

The route the train would take was not a direct one, but rather two adjoining sides of a square. Leaving Stuttgart, it was to head southeast, then cross over the *Danube* before crossing the German-Swiss border to back track southwest to Zurich.

There had been a minor problem. The railway gauge in Germany at that time had two main rail gauges, and in Switzerland there were three. A route had to be figured out that could accommodate the same gauge from start to finish, thus avoiding any transferring of the cargo. The final part of the journey to Nyon would take a further one hundred and twenty miles.

* * *

Known only to a chosen few, the Brent Depository at Nyon was in fact three stories in total, two above ground and the bottom one partly below. The deposit boxes were on the lowest floor. Access to the depository was by way of two lifts, one for normal daily use, and the second for use in the event of a power failure affecting the main lift; it was powered by the depository's own generator, which would cut in automatically in the event of failure to the main's supply. The lifts stood side-by-side; there were no stairs.

It was here that more than twenty percent of the ill-gotten gold and artifacts from Germany had been deposited during the last months before the end of World War II.

One reason depositors had chosen Brent was its unusual location. It was partly under the level of the lake, and therefore security was not as high as normally expected, with natural resources giving aid to the depository's own security.

One of the reasons this location had been selected was its inaccessibility. Another was that in the event of any form of attack on the depository, the lower part of the bank could be flooded; this would not do any harm to the gold, silver, jewellery, artifacts, or even any paintings, as the lake was a fresh water lake and anything that might be affected by flooding was sealed in watertight canisters, and even small drums.

*   *   *

Herman presented himself to the president of the Goldsworth Bank at 9:00am. the morning following the evening invasion on his home. Normally, Herman would have contacted the president on his return home once he had secured the explosive device, but it was the bank's strict policy that staff at 'any' level did not communicate out of office hours. Contacting the police was out of the question, at least until internal investigations could be mounted—another bank policy.

"Yes, Herman? What is it you wanted to see me about that's so important?"

"Well, sir, it's like this..." Herman went on to explain the events of the past fifteen hours.

*   *   *

Mario had removed all traces of his presence from his insurance company offices, which he had occupied earlier; he knew it would not be long before the police or the bank's investigators would arrive at the scene. Returning to his accommodation, he showered, changed, and placed his old clothes in a plastic bag. On his way out to dinner later in the day, he would drop off an article of clothing at each refuse bin he passed before proceeding to the Pelicana restaurant.

The Pelicana, again, was an ordinary looking building from the outside. Inside there were no frills, but the food was of unquestionable excellence.

On arrival at the restaurant, Mario ordered a pint of Carling lager, with an added dash of lime. While he waited for his drink, he glanced through the menu. When the waiter delivered his drink, Mario ordered the Chicken Kiev with Dauphinoise potatoes. He would reserve the choice of a sweet until he had completed his dinner.

While waiting for his main course to be delivered, Mario looked through the 'classified' adverts in the *London Evening Standard,* late edition.

It was no secret the underworld would advertise in the *Standard*. Everything was coded, of course. Although MI5 and Scotland Yard knew about this, neither they nor the police could prove anything.

Mario scribbled a half-dozen names and numbers on a napkin before placing the paper to one side.

Tomorrow looked to be an interesting day.

CHAPTER 4

I HAD NOT LONG RETURNED FROM making some discrete enquiries. A builder was having trouble obtaining payment for work he had carried out at said person's recently acquired house, a grad II listed building in a small Northampton village where alterations were strictly controlled by local authorities; in this case, the alterations were a completely new roof, twenty-two handmade windows, and three main outer doors, also handmade. This was due to the fact that the original windows and doors were not of a uniform size. I was about to draft a letter to the builder when the phone rang.

"Brian, its Henry," his deep voice bellowed down the line.

"Yes, Henry, and how are you today?"

"Fine, Brian, thank you. The Parkinson's accountant has suggested a meeting tomorrow at lunch time. He would like to know if that's okay, and if so, where?"

"Tomorrow's fine. Will you be joining us? If so, would you or he like to choose the venue?"

"If you'd like me to be there, that's not a problem."

"I think that might be a good idea, Henry, all things considered."

"Right, then. I'll let you know when and where later today, as soon as I've spoken to the person in question. Goodbye."

I replaced the receiver and went about my letter to the builder.

*   *   *

"Well, Herman. We seem to have gotten ourselves a bit of a problem, don't we?"

"Yes, sir. I'm afraid you're right—but honestly, what could I do?" Herman replied. "I was assured this money will be repaid, although I have my doubts. I would have called the police, but as you're aware, the bank's policy is to do nothing until internal affairs can investigate any similar matters first. I couldn't call you—again, the bank's policy, so my hands were somewhat tied."

"Quite right, Herman. Had you been able to call me last night, there was nothing we could do until now. You return to your desk and carry on as if nothing's happened. I'll take over from here."

Herman did just that.

The president picked up the phone and dialed a number.

"Ah, Henry, can you recommend a good PI? I might have the need for one."

"Yes, Max, as it so happens, I can."

*   *   *

Having been given directions to our lunch rendezvous, I met up with Henry slightly early.

23

"Hello, Brian, me boy," Henry greeted as I entered the 'Shepherd and Flock' public house. He had been seated near the door, so as not to miss me. Walter Prendigast had not yet arrived.

"What would you like to drink?" Henry enquired.

"Half a pint of lager," I told Henry. "*Stella,* if they have it."

Henry brought my drink to the table and sat back down.

"Before our friend arrives, I may have another job for you," Henry told me.

"Sounds interesting. At this rate, I'm going to have to open another office," I jokingly replied.

"Yes, well the president of the Swiss-owned Goldsworth Bank in London has a small problem—possibly not so small."

"Go on," I prompted.

"Well, it's all rather strange, really; Max Hofer, the president of the bank, will be able to tell you better. What I can tell you is that the bank was robbed of four million GBP in a most unusual way! My client is currently employing what he calls a 'top notch' security firm but feels his particular problem may well fall outside their expertise."

It was at this moment Walter Prendigast arrived.

I had never met Walter while I was working at Parkinson's; the nearest I ever got to him was his signature on my pay slip every month.

He was a person of slim build. He was also tall, which extenuated his overall appearance. Recognising Henry, Walter came over to our table. Pulling out the only empty chair, he sat down and introduced himself.

"So you're Brian Ridley," he said as I stood up to greet him. "Indeed a pleasure to meet you. I'm sorry I couldn't be of any help during your crisis with Parkinson's meats in Longborough a few years ago. I wasn't in a position to do anything, really."

"That's okay," I said. "I quite understand."

Henry called the bartender over for Walter to order a drink. After the barman left, Walter went on to explain why he felt the Parkinsons were laundering money and added that he sincerely hoped he was wrong.

"My first sense of something not quite normal was the fact that invoices for 'goods in' didn't match those of 'goods out'. Then later I recalled the printing press used by Parkinson junior, for the purpose of carrying out his counterfeiting, was never recovered."

"So what is it, basically, you're saying?" I asked.

"Quite simply that the Parkinsons are still printing money, selling it on the black market—where there are plenty of buyers—and using the proceeds to pay for their purchases, thus saving their own money!"

"A wild idea," Henry commented, "but certainly plausible. Particularly in this day and age of high-tech printing and advanced crime!"

"I have to agree," I commented. "But don't you think that's a little more than risky?"

"Yes, but why did Parkinson junior get involved with counterfeiting in the first place if the family fortunes were still intact?"

"As I heard it while I was at the factory, it wasn't the Parkinson estate that was in financial difficulty, but Parkinson junior himself, miss managing his part of the empire in Longborough."

"What is it you would like us to do?" Henry asked Walter.

"Maybe someone could tail Parkinson senior, see where he goes, what he does. I have to tell you, I can't work for a company that's carrying on illegal financial operations."

"What do you think, Brian?" Henry asked.

"Well, Henry, I do recall a good friend of mine, an ex-colleague whom I visited on my return from Libya. He gave me some valuable information regarding the Parkinson Empire. The purpose was to help me make the decision whether or not to accept employment with them. He told me their chief accountant was leaving, as he suspected there were suspicious financial dealings going on. I believe our friend here took over soon after this guy left."

"So what do you think?" Henry repeated.

"Well, Henry, I'm not very experienced in shadowing people; I believe that's the expression. I'm not sure if that would get us anywhere anyway. What I suggest is that if Walter here can give us information on the companies the Parkinsons do business with, between us we might discover more than we might by tailing anyone."

"I'm inclined to agree," Henry chipped in.

"If that gets us nowhere, then may I also suggest you contact the income tax people in Caxton," I continued. "At least that way you'll cover yourself, and they're in a better position to make the necessary enquiries than we are. One thing I do find rather disturbing, we now have two senior accountants, one who was, and now one who is very concerned with the financial activities surrounding the Parkinson Empire."

CHAPTER 5

MARIO GLANCED AT THE CLOCK on the wall of his miniscule bed-sit. It was showing 9:30am; time to make some phone calls. This he would do from the small town of Milton Ernest, three miles up the A6 from Bedford town centre. But first he would have a light breakfast of ham and eggs, washed down with a cup of English breakfast tea.

*   *   *

Earlier in the year, Mario had been doing some research about the Brent depository on the northern shore of Lake Geneva.

He had opened a medium-sized deposit box as a means of checking the depository facilities. In it he had placed twenty thousand Swiss francs (a little over thirteen thousand pounds) to help finance the Swiss side of his operation. The 4.1 million GB pounds would arrive after doing the rounds in the next three to four days.

During this time, Mario had learned that the two small towers at the upper level were in fact a pair of air vents; this was to allow for a speedier flooding of the lower floor in an emergency. He had also learned that the lower floor housed 357 deposit boxes, 190 small, 100 medium, and 67 large. It was considered that half of the boxes were owned by persons who were no longer living.

At the same time, Mario had drawn up a list of necessary items for his forthcoming exercise. From this he would assemble a group of required 'operators'.

It was this list Mario was looking at while finishing his breakfast.

*   *   *

I was again in my office when Henry telephoned me.

"Hello, Henry," I said. "Have you heard from Mr. Prendigast?"

"No, not yet. I'm calling concerning another matter."

"Oh, what that might be Henry?" I asked with modest curiosity.

"I've had a call from a Mr. Max Hoffer, the president of the Goldsworth Bank in north London I was telling you about. He asked me for your telephone number."

"Henry, why would the president of an international bank in London like Goldsworth need to get in touch with me?"

"Not you, so much as a good PI. Make your mark, Brian me boy, and stay near the phone if you can. I think you'll get a call shortly."

"Thank you, Henry. I'll keep you posted."

About fifty minutes later, the phone rang.

"Good morning. My name is Max Hoffer, president of the Swiss Goldsworth Bank in London. I would like to speak to a Mr. Ridley if that's possible, please."

"That's me, sir."

"One of our solicitors recommended you to us and gave me your telephone number. Are you in a position to come to London tomorrow morning, Mr. Ridley?"

"I can do that, sir. Any particular time?"

"Say mid-day. I'll buy you lunch after our meeting."

Mid-day sounds like a very familiar time, I thought, reflecting back to my regular trips to MI5, and then MI6.

"I'll be at your bank at mid-day sharp tomorrow morning, Mr. Hoffer."

"Thank you, Mr Ridley. I look forward to meeting you. Good day."

I telephoned Henry to let him know I had spoken to Max Hoffer and that I would be meeting with him tomorrow late morning.

"Did you wish to accompany me?" I asked Henry.

"No, me boy; the matter is investigative, not legal, but do let me know how you get on. I'll be most interested."

"I will," I promised Henry.

*   *   *

Mario sat in a cubicle near the window of the George and Dragon public house, sipping a gin and tonic. He was to meet a fellow by the name of Ian Brown, if that was his real name—not that Mario cared. Mr. Brown was a lock expert specialising in the field of 'electronic' locking systems, in particular the one used by the Brent Depository in Switzerland.

In times past, Mario used to pass the time of day studying passers-by and guessing what they did for a living. Of course, there was no way of knowing if he had ever guessed correctly; however, on this occasion he was certain he had found Ian Brown as he headed towards the entrance of the pub, wearing a yellow T-shirt with a red collar, black jogging trousers and white trainers. What Mario considered was the giveaway were the bi-focal glasses. It was for this reason Mario had sat by the window. On this occasion, he had unquestionably guessed right.

*   *   *

I arrived at the Goldsworth Bank well before mid-day. After passing security, I presented myself to the reception clerk.

"Good morning, Mr Hines," I said, seeing the nameplate on the front of his desk. "I have an appointment to see Mr Hoffer at mid-day.

"Wait one moment, please. I'll let him know you're here."

While I waited, I took in my surroundings. Very much unlike British Banks, the Goldsworth Bank was light, airy and modern, whereas traditional British high street banks were dark, with lots of dark stained teak and South African Mahogany; rather foreboding.

A few moments later, Mr. Hines was back and asked if I would please be good enough to follow him.

Max Hoffer looked every bit the role of a bank president, wearing a charcoal grey three-piece suit, pale blue shirt and a slightly darker blue tie. Below his dark hair sat a pair of bi-focal glasses. His office, however, was quite unlike the central part of the bank, somewhat darker, with many paintings in gold frames. I guessed most of them were originals; in some cases, pictures of presidents past, I guessed. The room was long and narrow. At one end was a gilt-edged desk with green-leather insert in the middle. Behind it was a high-backed chair, also with gilt trimmings. In the centre of the room was a glass-topped table, three chairs on each side and one at each end, giving the appearance of a small board room setting.

It was at this table Max Hoffer invited me to sit, while at the same time calling his vice president on his intercom.

"I've asked our vice president to join us," Max Hoffer informed me. "You'll soon see why."

I had to admit to being slightly mystified. Max asked if we would like a drink during the debate; I opted for a lemon and soda. Once we were seated, Max Hoffer nodded to Herman, who started to tell his story.

"Two days ago, while returning home from the office..." Herman commenced, and thirty-five minutes later he finished his story. He had been quite detailed in his deliverance.

"What chance did I have?" he exploded. "An unbelievable experience, I can tell you. My wife has had to cancel all her concert appearances as a result. She's a concert pianist, you understand; she's really shaken up by it all."

While Herman was telling his story, I was making a few notes.

"Do you have any video surveillance tapes?" I asked Mr. Hoffer, at which point he picked up the phone.

"Security, this is Max Hoffer. Do we have video surveillance tapes for the last forty-eight hours?"

There was a slight pause, I presumed while security checked.

"Yes, sir," came the eventual reply.

"Good, then I'm sending my vice president down to you with an investigating officer. The time period we're looking at is..." Mr. Hoffer cupped his hand over the mouthpiece and looked at Herman. "What time period are we talking about exactly?"

"Between 7:00pm and 8:00pm," Herman replied.

Max Hoffer relayed the information to security.

On our arrival, one story below ground level, Herman used his key-card to enter the small security control room. Along the far wall was a set of monitors. Two were turned on. We were informed there were two cameras in operation the previous evening, one covering the general area outside of the building, and one covering the area just inside of the main doors.

One of the security guards indicated for us to be seated and replayed the tape of the previous evening, starting at four-times forward speed. The clock in the top right hand corner was also going at four-times normal time. It was a split screen, the left side showing the outside and the right side showing the inside.

Suddenly, two men appeared outside of the main entrance doors. The security guard immediately slowed down the video to normal. The lighting was not very good. With only the street lights outside and the dim security lighting inside, it was almost impossible to recognise either man. Herman informed us he was the one in front. He was seen to cancel the lock timer and enter, followed by the second man. Only by this information could it be deemed that the second man was the criminal. The picture was not very good at all, not only due to the poor lighting, but also because the second man purposely kept his head low.

"Can you zoom in on the second man?" I asked.

The picture instantly went to twice the size. Because of the poor lighting and magnification, it was not possible to decipher the second man at all; in fact, it could have been a woman, but for the fact that the vice president had said otherwise.

"Is it possible to have a copy of the tape?" I asked. "I know someone who may be able to enhance the picture somewhat."

"Yes, but we'll have to check with the president of the bank first."

Before leaving to join Max Hoffer for lunch and eventually go back to Bedford, I had requested copies of both the original opening account and the loan account. The opening account, I had been told, was a numbered account and therefore gave up little information. The loan account, however, had business addresses and phone numbers. Again, I felt sure our villain would by now be disconnected and long gone. For what it was worth, a description of the villain was also supplied, as presented to the bank by both Herman and his wife.

What I found a little more than unusual was the fact that our villain had 'insisted' this was a loan and would be repaid. The question, therefore, was what was the man guilty of if he repaid the money?

It could be breaking and entering; however, technically he was invited—wasn't he? Threatening with menaces, possibly, but then as it turned out, the laptop computer was in fact quite harmless. Also, the culprit had given Herman the telephone 'sender', which turned out to be a normal and harmless mobile phone. And before driving off, he had shown Herman that the gold Walther PP was empty! This got me to thinking that our villain did in fact intend to repay the money; by what means, though, I hadn't a clue.

Once back in the office, I would make some enquiries. My first priority was to see about improving the quality of the videotape. Tomorrow, I would visit both premises of 'Homes & Autos' insurance. If nothing else, I could hopefully talk to the owners of the neighbouring properties.

*   *   *

Mario had told Ian Brown only what he needed to know. At the depository in question, there were three different size boxes, small, medium, and large, but they all had the same double 'butterfly' key locking configuration as the key securing system for the boxes. Mario had brought back a diagram taken from his own deposit box, plus an imprint of his key. The measurements were accurate to within half a millimeter; they had to be, for obvious reasons. Mario seriously hoped to bring back a mental imprint of the 'other' key when he collected his Swiss francs. Ian Brown's job was to produce a rechargeable, battery-operated electronic key box. This needed to be watertight; Mario had made this quite clear. A substitute for the two male keys had to be placed in the key holes by the two individuals at the same time, likewise turned simultaneously. The hard part was for Ian to work out the configuration of the master key so the unit could be used where it needed to be on all 357 boxes, even with possible help from Mario and a sketch of the master key. One thing Mario knew was that both keys were the same size, so figuring out a master suit shouldn't be too difficult for an expert; making the electronic box, though, might be.

It was possible that the larger boxes would be left untouched—be a second priority—as would some, if not most of the gold bars plundered from some of the European Banks. This would ultimately depend on the time factor.

CHAPTER 6

I T WAS 8:45AM, AND I was checking the morning's mail. I had received the promised information from Parkinson's accountant. The companies Parkinson supplied were quite impressive, many more than when I was employed by them several years ago. There was a long list of high street supermarkets, as well as several respected catering firms. One of my first tasks was to visit a couple of these places and see for myself the quality and prices of the various products. I selected two of the top five on the list Parkinson's accountant had supplied.

My second task was to consider employing an assistant.

At 10:30am on the dot, I arrived at the first supermarket on my list. I had carefully arranged the order of my two visits in accordance with the locations and other work for the day. This had been helped greatly by the aid of a local map of the area.

I was extremely impressed with most of the produce on display, in particular the prices showing on the Parkinson labels by comparison to other brands. I bought a sirloin beef steak, large enough for both me and Christina, from one supermarket, and pork sausages from another. I was already familiar with the quality of Parkinson's pork and lamb from way back when I was their chief and only engineer. These Christina and I would have over the next couple of days; this was to assess the quality of the meat, in an attempt to try and determine the profitability of Parkinson as a company. As I recalled from several years ago, the quality of the Parkinson products was good—was it still as good? Were they now cost cutting as a means of getting sales, therefore needing to find other sources of income to balance the books?

* * *

Later in the day, I drove to 'Homes & Autos' in Bedford, as it was the nearest of the two offices. As expected, it was closed. A sign on the door said they were closed for two weeks' holiday. The end of November seemed to be a strange time to be taking a holiday of two weeks, unless whoever was running the shop was taking a holiday to a warmer climate. Why both shops at the same time? Unless, of course, it was a family-run business.

It was a double fronted shop. I peered through the windows on each side of the entrance. It didn't look deserted; in fact, it looked quite the opposite. It looked like what the sign on the door said. The next door to the right led to a 'Red Cross' charity shop, and to the left was a hardware store. I checked my voice-activated micro tape recorder in my breast pocket and went into the charity shop first.

"The office next door," I enquired to the lady behind the counter. "The sign on the door said they're closed for two weeks' holiday, but there are no dates on the information to say when they'll re-open. Can you tell me if you know when they'll open again?" I asked.

"I believe the end of next week," she told me.

"Do you know how long they've been open?" I continued.

"About a month, maybe a little longer."

Again, I thought it odd they were on vacation so soon after opening.

"I don't suppose you know who the owner is?" I persisted.

"Yes, this whole row of shops is owned by an investment company, and the occupiers have a lease. I only know this as we're a charity, and as such we have a concession on the amount of rent we pay."

I thanked the lady and left, not wishing to push my luck.

I entered the hardware store next. Inside, the storekeeper was stocking one of the shelves.

"Can you tell me anything about the insurance office next door?" I asked as he rose from a crouching position.

"Such as?" he asked.

I repeated what I had asked the lady in the charity shop and received similar answers. One thing I did ask that I hadn't in the charity shop was if the gentleman running the hardware store ever got a chance to recognise the owner of the insurance company next door.

"Not really," he replied. "You see, whenever I did see the person in question, he was always in a charcoal coloured overcoat, a similar coloured scarf wrapped around his neck and the lower half of his face. He had dark rimmed glasses and wore a hat pulled low over his forehead. It *is* late November."

Well, that didn't tell me anything.

Next I visited Northampton. Again with the help of a map, I found the other 'Homes & Autos', not surprisingly with a similar notice on the door. It still occurred to me that it was a little more than strange—both branches closed at the same time? And after being in operation for such a short while?

The result of my enquiries was similar to that in Bedford, with one exception: I got a decent description of the gentleman managing the business. To the right of 'Homes & Autos' was a blank plot of land. To the left was a laundry cum dry cleaners shop. When I entered, a bell rang above the door. As I approached the counter, a middle aged lady came from the back of the shop to greet me.

"Yes, sir, what can I do for you?" she enquired.

"I'm moving to this area," I lied. "The company next door was going to insure my new house contents, but I see they're closed and wondered if you could help me?"

"In what way can I be of help, sir?"

"When will they re-open?"

Again, I received a similar answer to the one I got in Bedford.

"I don't expect you could describe the owner for me?" I asked.

She gave me a wry look, as if to say, *Don't you know?*

I smiled.

"He was a man, in his mid-forties, receding dark hair with a bald patch in the middle, and of average height. He was wearing gold rimmed glasses. I only know because he came into the shop with some laundry; that, I considered to be most interesting. It led me to believe that he might not be married. I gave the lady my name and telephone number, asking her if she would give me a call when the insurance office reopened. She kindly agreed."

Back in the office, I removed the mini tape recorder and replayed my conversations from the beginning, at the same time making a few notes.

*　　*　　*

Mario was sitting in his favourite cafe, having just had breakfast. He was now enjoying his second cup of tea while at the same time going through last night's *London Evening Standard*. He had recruited Ian Brown as the second member of his team—Mario being the first—an expert, among other things, in computer technology. He was now looking for a guy by the name of Nick Burrows, described as a 'top man' in alarm systems. Mario considered he would not have much trouble with the alarms. He was coming in from the lake side, just below the water line, but he needed to be prepared. He needed advice from an expert *and* for one to be on hand *if* needed.

Flooding the lower level would need the vent valves to be opened, which was why Mario needed Nick Burrows. Flooding without the vent valves open would cause too much air to escape into the lake, something Mario would rather like to avoid.

*　　*　　*

I had completed my notes regarding the Goldsworth Bank affair, using the system that had worked for me splendidly before over many years, even way back when I was in junior management: a list of for, and a list of against.

These had added notes into the margin. I would concentrate on the longer of the two lists, which turned out to be the list against.

I picked up the phone and dialed the Goldsworth Bank. I needed to bring Max Hoffer up to date on what little I had discovered so far.

"This is the Goldsworth Bank," a lady who I took to be the receptionist answered.

"This is Mr. Ridley calling. I need to speak to Max Hoffer, if that's at all possible."

"Wait a moment, please, while I try to contact him."

Office institutions were so obvious in their telephone communications; they expected callers to hang on their every word. The lady in reception knew exactly where Mr Hoffer was—it was her job to know! A few minutes later, Max Hoffer came on the line.

"Mr. Ridley, good to hear from you."

"Likewise, Mr. Hoffer. I'd like to bring you up to date on your missing four million GBP," I told him. "Would you like me to come to the bank, or do you favour any alternative communication?"

"No, by all means, do visit the bank; I think it's better that way."

"Is tomorrow possible?" I enquired.

"Tomorrow, then. Join me for lunch again, say between twelve and half past," Max Hoffer said.

"I look forward to it," I replied and replaced the receiver.

I now proceeded to make my report to the accountant of Parkinson meats.

Investigations into the company, with the help of the Internet, revealed that the factory in Kirby, the one that Mr. Parkinson, Jr. had been managing, was to close with a hundred percent redundancies. This I found to be a little odd, as the factory was brand new and purposely designed with the latest freezing technologies slightly more than four years ago. I was not sure if this was due to the fact that Parkinson, Jr. was now in prison, but I was certain Percival Parkinson could have found a manager for the plant if he needed to; there were several loyal departmental managers at Caxton, leaving Percival to oversee the Kirby plant.

Something was definitely not quite right.

I phoned Henry to bring him up to date on the events of both cases.

*   *   *

Nick Burrows was studying the *Racing Times* when his phone rang.

"Yes, who's calling?"

"Ah, Mr. Burrows, would you be interested in a small but nonetheless quite profitable job?" Petri replied without giving his name.

"I could be. When?"

"In about three weeks' time," Mario replied.

"Yes, I can be available; I'm tied up at the moment, though. Maybe you can call me nearer the time you're ready?"

"I will do that," Mario Petri informed Mr. Burrows, then ended the call.

Petri was not concerned about flood water escaping into the bank area outside of the depository section. A two-foot thick circular door, six feet in diameter with a weight of sixteen tons and twelve two-inch cylinder locks around its circumference, separated the depository from the rest of the bank. It was watertight! Only after the holiday when the bank re-opened would the alarm sound when they tried to open the vault door.

*   *   *

I arrived at the Goldsworth Bank just like before at the appointed time and presented myself to the reception desk; not Arthur Hines this time, but instead a lady. The clock on the wall was showing exactly half past twelve.

"Mr. Ridley to see Mr. Hoffer," I told the young lady.

"One moment, please."

A few moments later, Mr. Hoffer came up to the reception desk.

"Let's go straight to lunch," he said. "We can talk there."

Over lunch, I brought Max Hoffer up to date on my enquiries thus far. I told him what I knew, then what I thought I knew, and then finally what I didn't know. I informed him that the video had been enhanced with some modest success. But there was no chance of recognising the person accompanying the vice president; most of the time, the view was blocked by the vice president. I mentioned that the lady in the dry cleaners next door to the Northamptonshire office gave a similar description of the man in question as Herman's wife gave. I then followed up with what I considered to be some sound advice.

"I do think it's in your best interest to report this incident to the police. They are in a much better position to discover the whereabouts of this criminal. We can give them a description, vague though it is, which they can circulate throughout the whole country. I can still work on the case in the background, if you so wish."

Max leaned into the table and spoke with his knife and fork poised in mid-air.

"I'm not so sure Herman is telling us everything quite as it happened," he half-whispered. "I'd like to wait just a little while longer, if you don't mind."

"Not at all. I'll continue discreet enquiries and report to you twice a week until you tell me otherwise, if that's all right."

CHAPTER 7

A FEW DAYS AFTER HIS FIRST call, Mario spoke to Nick Burrows for the second time. He wanted to know for sure the man was familiar with the alarm systems that were fitted at the Brent depository. He hadn't needed to give Burrows the name of the depository. He already knew the systems in place; this, he had researched several months earlier. The systems were three in total.

First, there was the heat sensitivity alarm. It could recognise any change in temperature within two degrees of the upper two floors. Then there were the floor sensors, capable of responding to any weight increase of more than four grams, again on the upper two floors. Finally, there were the lasers, criss-crossed along the lower half of the lower floor, up to the front of the massive vault door.

The lasers were of Swiss manufacture. Only four had been fitted into banks or similar institutions, three in Switzerland, and one in Austria. They were manufactured by Ziemdeck. The technical specifications and circuitry were a closely kept secret to prevent unofficial prying eyes. Unfortunately, Mario was unable to get any blueprints of the system. This was another reason for getting into the lower section from the lake side. The first two systems were now standard fittings in most depositories and banks.

The other thing Mario needed to know was if there were any alarms that would sound if the basement was flooded. Apparently, the answer was no. Mario didn't think the other alarms in the main building would be a problem, as he would not be coming in from the front. But it didn't hurt to have all the information available.

*　　*　　*

Christina and I were enjoying the Parkinson's sirloin steak, accompanied with Brussel sprouts, English runner beans, and baby newt potatoes. We had both eaten Parkinson's meat on many occasions before when I was the chief engineer at Parkinson's processing plant in Longborough, but this was premium grade 'A', whereas before when I was working at the Parkinson factory, I was only allowed to take home the 'end of run leftovers'.

Chris had known I had been 'secretly' re-employed by the Parkinson's company accountant, this time on a self-employed basis. What had only just occurred to me was the fact that Walter Prendigast was himself quite capable of carrying out the exercise I had just carried out, so why hadn't he? Was it a case of attack being better than defence? I came to the conclusion that I would have to look at this from a different perspective. I would contact Henry tomorrow and tell him my thoughts on the matter.

The following day, after calling Henry, I was told by his secretary that he was unavailable, but nonetheless she would see that he would call me back when he returned. His secretary added that he was expected to be in court most of the day. I, in turn, assured her there was no urgency.

I made my slightly overdue return visit to 'Homes & Autos' in Bedford; as I expected, the office was still closed, with the same notice stuck on the inside of the door. On my return to the office, I checked through the notes I had made on my first visit to 'Homes & Autos'. I would contact Max Hoffer tomorrow and make my half-weekly report, as promised; however, there wasn't much to report.

*   *   *

Mario Petri had not long returned from France and Switzerland. He had been getting updates crucial to the next part of his operation. He had been staying at the hotel *Le Lac Leman,* not far from the rather charming town of Yvoire, on the southern shores of Lake Geneva. There were several reasons for his visit, the utmost being the importance of timing. He had put a lot of effort and planning into this operation—and now, a lot of money.

Several months ago, Mario had made arrangements to purchase a twenty-nine metre exploration boat, the *Senator Explorer,* complete with a two man submersible, the *FNRS,* a twin four bladed HD battery-operated machine. It had just completed a recent four-month charter on Lake Geneva.

The *Senator Explorer* was built in 1980. Most of the superstructure was in the forward ten metres of the vessel, the bridge with the equipment control room and laboratory below, with accommodation for eight aft of the control room, a small but well fitted galley and a mess room for eating. The submersible took up a large part of the rest of the deck space mid and aft, along with the lowering crane, compressors and other necessary support machinery. The submersible, the *FNRS,* was a little over sixteen metres long. As was standard practice with this design of submersible, any payload was transported in wire baskets on the port and starboard side, mounted outside of the vessel. Fitted on the nose of the submersible was a triple head three-foot diameter Derision rotary boring tool, which could be used vertically or horizontally. In this instance, the boring tool would be used in the horizontal position. The boring process was greatly assisted by the vibration generated by the tool. With a three-foot opening, the divers would need to temporarily remove their oxygen bottles before entering, replacing them once inside. Two individual sets of batteries were fitted, one set of ten x 24v dc Lifepo4'—for powering the drill head— and a second similar set-up for powering the engines. Both the batteries and the drill head were of Chinese origin.

*   *   *

Nearing the end of the Second World War, a ferry, the *Morning Mist,* had left the port of Montreux secretly carrying gold, heading for Versoix in Switzerland. Thought to be quicker and safer than by road or rail, it was presumed she sank, as she never arrived at her appointed destination. There were no survivors. Because of this, it was never recorded as to where the vessel sank. Nobody had ever managed to find the sunken treasure. It was never discovered how or why she sank. Many believed a bomb had been planted on board, timed to go off halfway into her destination. Remote detonators were unheard of at this time. Because she sailed late, it was also believed the bomb had gone off before she was halfway to her destination, not the deepest part of the lake. Over the last fifty years, vast inroads had been made in underwater exploration and electronic investigative technology. This is what the *Senator Explorer* had been trying to achieve over the last few months. If reports were anywhere near accurate, the present value of the gold was twenty-three million dollars! Unfortunately, the *Senator Explorer* had not been successful in finding the lost treasure.

The vessel was now available for sale, at a price of one million-seven-hundred thousand euro's. The *Senator Explorer* had been based at the Nerier basin on the French border of Lake Geneva and was now anchored in Lake Leman—part of lake Geneva, only a short boat ride from the hotel Mario was staying at. He had decided to purchase the vessel rather than charter it. He did not need a crew; he would find one for himself, as he would for the submersible. The importance of timing was also crucial to coincide with the Swiss Easter holiday during the middle of March, giving him four full days to carry out his mission.

While Mario was in France, he decided to cross the border into Switzerland, only five miles across the lake from his hotel, and check his deposit box at the Brent depository a short distance from Nyon. This gave him a chance for a last-minute observation of the building in case of any possible changes, as well as to pinpoint the exact point of entry, withdraw his money, and have a final look at the master key. The depository was ideally placed for his operation, on a very small peninsular jutting out into the lake.

Two specially designed submersible extraction pumps were assembled at the outer wall, as were the electro-pneumatic flooding valves. It was at this point where Mario would make his entrance.

Once back in England, Mario was ready to put the final stages of his operation together. This included the fourth person of the group he now called his team, the submersible operator.

Mario knew a guy from his early days in the Royal Navy. The man's name was Eddy Grant; this was all he could remember. He had been serving on submarines as a leading hand. His service HQ had been the shore base of *H.M.S Dolphin*, a little outside of Portsmouth harbour, known as the number one submarine base, well known by the locals for its one-hundred foot tall diving tower. This was also used by the trainee divers at the nearby diving school of *H.M.S. Vernon.*

Eddy had been dishonourably discharged from the Navy for stealing solid silver cutlery from the officer's mess, both on the submarine and *H.M.S. Dolphin*. He had made a spare time occupation of making tie-pins, cuff links, and other similar jewelry from the solid silver cutlery. Although Mario only knew him briefly, he was confident he would not be hard to track down.

Mario was confident Eddy knew all that was needed to man the *FNRS*.

It was getting quite late in the day, so Mario decided to track down Eddy Grant tomorrow.

*   *   *

As Mario suspected, Eddy Grant was not difficult to find. This was greatly helped by the fact that Eddy had been dishonourably discharged from the Royal Navy for charges of theft. It was one thing stealing from your boss, but something else when it came to stealing from the government; because of this, the authorities had been keeping a close watch on him. A call to them enquiring of his whereabouts with an offer of employment resulted in Mario obtaining a phone number, along with an address. The officials in question were only too happy to cooperate, in view of the chances that Eddy may have a chance of going straight and getting a legitimate job.

Mario called Eddy; when Eddy answered the call, he sounded a little nervous. Mario introduced himself and explained that he knew him from earlier days. He then told Eddy he had a job for him if he was interested.

Eddy indicated he was.

Mario only told Eddy the job was in Switzerland and to be available in about three weeks' time.

CHAPTER 8

IT WAS A LITTLE PAST mid-day when Henry called.

"How are you, Henry?" I enquired.

"Fine. A little tired; three days in court. Court cases are always tiring. And you?"

"Likewise, fine," I replied.

"My secretary has informed me you telephoned yesterday. I didn't get out of court until late. The judge wanted to round things up before the end of the day."

"That's okay. I did tell your secretary it wasn't urgent. I need to bring you up to date with the latest situation regarding the Parkinsons, as well as that of the Goldsworth Bank."

"Are you able to come up to Caxton tomorrow?" Henry asked.

"Yes, I can do that. When?" I asked.

"Late morning," Henry replied. "Then I'll buy you lunch."

"That'll be nice. Thank you, Henry. See you tomorrow, then. Bye."

I couldn't remember the last time I had been treated to so many lunches in such a short period of time.

Next I phoned Max Hoffer to give him the twice weekly update, although there was little to offer. I told him that what few leads I had were all dried up; our man had been more than cleaver in covering his tracks. I further suggested reporting the incident to the police. They would be able to gain legal access to both insurance offices for possible fingerprints, as well as carry out some not so discrete enquiries.

*   *   *

Mario was looking for one more person to complete his team; someone quite versatile, someone who could fill in all the gaps. A person who could assist Eddy Grant in the submersible, while at the same time support those in the depository—when needed.

He decided to contact Ian Brown first, then the other two later if necessary, to see if they knew of anybody who may fit the bill.

Ian Brown didn't know of anyone off-hand, but if he thought of anyone, he would contact Mario immediately.

Mario was not prepared to wait. He contacted Nick Burrows, who informed him he knew of two persons who might be able to help; however, as it turned out, the two people Nick had in mind were unavailable.

As a last resort, Mario contacted Eddy Grant.

"As it happens, I have an ex-Navy friend who might be able to help. Give me twenty-four hours, and I'll get back to you."

*   *   *

I met up with Henry a little before mid-day at the same public house where I'd previously met the Parkinsons' accountant. The restaurant part was beginning to get quite busy with the usual lunch time visitors.

"Good to see you, Henry."

"Likewise, me boy."

"So you had a full day yesterday." It was a statement rather than a question.

"Yes, you could say that, and the two days before," he replied in a somewhat exhausted tone. "Long days in court are getting a little tiring for me, and the last few days have been unusually warm for this time of year."

"I understand what you're saying, Henry, and I sympathise with you. I remember our court case in Northampton, and that was an autumn day."

The waiter—or barman, I wasn't sure which—came over to our table. We ordered drinks and asked for the menu. After ordering shrimp and crab savory fried rice for me—I was still keeping an eye on my weight—and steamed fish and creamed mashed potatoes with marrowfat peas for Henry, we got down to business.

"So what's the latest?" Henry enquired.

"Well, while looking into the Parkinson affair, it occurred to me that our friend Mr. Prendigast could easily have carried out the same exercise I did. So why call in outside help? I considered perhaps it was a case of attack is better than defense. So, I went and looked up the Parkinson Company on the Internet."

"And?"

"An interesting situation has developed. Shortly after my demise from the Parkinsons a few years ago, the factory Parkinson Jr. was controlling moved to a purpose built meat processing factory seven miles away."

"And?" Henry repeated.

"They are to close with 100% redundancies, seventy employees. What do you think of that?" I asked.

"Most enlightening," Henry replied while adjusting his napkin.

"Yes, this was not only a purpose built factory, it had the latest in blast freezing, temperature-controlled storage and high-tech vacuum packaging. I know this, as I was in the process of 'setting it all up' before I was dismissed. What do you think?" I asked Henry.

"Indeed, what do I think? I think we should have a word with Mr. Prendigast, that's what I think."

"Right, well there is a little change in the Goldsworth Bank situation; I updated Max Hoffer on events after you called yesterday afternoon, and I suggested calling in the police for the reasons I explained. He was quite insistent, though, that I hold off. He felt his vice president was holding back information, so I agreed. He's promised to get back to me later this afternoon."

* * *

Mario was in one of his favorite cafés, the *Greasy Spoon*. It was mid-morning, and he had just finished 'brunch'. The café was fast becoming his office. He had just received word from Eddy that he had found the extra guy Mario had asked for. His name was Collin Write. Eddy added that he could vouch for him. Mario had to smile to himself; after all, he really was not the best person to vouch for anybody when it came to anyone's character.

Mario glanced at his watch; 11:00am. Tuesday, the 3rd of March. He looked out of the window; the weather was blustery and still cold.

Removing his notes from the briefcase sitting on the chair beside him, he looked to see what was next on his programme.

He ordered yet another coffee.

He and Eddy Grant needed to be on the *Senator Explorer* sometime on Sunday 16th March, and the other three at the Hotel *Le Lac Leman* ready to be transferred to the survey vessel the following day. This allowed them until the afternoon on Thursday the 19th to get acquainted with the vessel and its equipment and do a couple of 'dry runs' before the four day long Easter weekend bank holiday, starting at 4:30pm on Thursday. Mario knew this, as he had seen the customer information notice on his recent visit to the depository.

* * *

Henry called to say he had set up a meeting for mid-day with Walter Prendigast at the same public house as before, and he apologized for the short notice.

"Not a problem," I said. "I can be there."

I proceeded to download, then print out the information regarding the closure of the Parkinson factory in Kirby. This I would take to our meeting with Walter Prendigast. The sophisticated, up market equipment and machinery was to be auctioned in about three weeks' time—the exact date to be confirmed—and not transferred to any other factory in the group; again, rather strange.

As before, Henry was sitting at a corner table when I arrived, and Walter had not yet made his presence. I sat down in one of the vacant chairs after Henry stood up to greet me.

"Glad you could make it," he said.

I gave Henry the downloaded printout regarding the Parkinson factory closure in Kirby. He looked at it with seemingly mild surprise.

"Walter made no mention of this at our last meeting," Henry exclaimed.

"Quite," I replied. "I find it hard to believe that as the company's accountant, he had no idea the Kirby plant was to close, especially as there would be, among other things, redundancy payments to calculate."

I nodded to Henry. At that moment, Walter Prendigast entered the public house. We both stood up as an indication to Walter as to where we were sitting. He came over to us. Once seated, Henry beckoned to the barman to order drinks. While we waited for our drinks to arrive, I told Walter about my visit to the two supermarkets and my purpose for doing so. After our drinks arrived, Henry presented Walter with the photocopy of the information I had downloaded regarding the Parkinsons at Kirby.

"I didn't know anything about this until yesterday afternoon," he commented. "There was a board meeting that didn't finish until quite late; otherwise, I would have called you."

"Well, according to the information here, it would appear they're going to auction off most of the equipment on site in a little over three weeks' time and not transfer it to any other site."

"Yes, again, I know only from the meeting yesterday," Walter replied.

"As the senior accountant at the Parkinsons', you did not know about the closure of an almost new factory?" I felt compelled to ask again.

"Why do you think the Parkinsons are closing the Kirby factory?" Henry asked. "Do you think it has anything to do with Parkinson Jr.'s imprisonment?"

"I don't know," Walter replied. "I'll try and find out and let you know."

"That would be helpful," I replied. "And I would seriously consider getting in touch with the tax people," I added.

Walter got up to leave, seemingly quite nervous.

"I have another meeting," he declared. "I have to go. I'll let you know as soon as I hear anything of importance; of that, I promise."

With that, he left.

I looked at Henry; he looked back, eyebrows raised.

"Something isn't quite right here," he said.

"I'm definitely inclined to agree with you," I replied.

After lunch, I returned to the office, feeling there were more unanswered questions than before lunch. I also felt that if Walter contacted the taxman, he was in the clear; if he didn't, he would become my number one suspect—that's if there was anything to suspect.

CHAPTER 9

MARIO WAS SITTING IN HIS bed-sit, going over the final details for the second part of his plan. He needed to contact his four team members with instructions as to when and where to meet. He still had to meet Collin Write, having taken him on at Eddy's suggestion, but time was running out. Mario had agreed on a price for each person based on their individual merits, then informed them that they would be paid irrespective of the success or failure of the operation; ten percent when they arrived in France, the remainder upon completion of the operation before they left France. He had further explained that the gains were not his, but those of a company of men who were financing the entire operation. But, he added, a bonus *might* be forthcoming if all went well and according to plan.

Mario had given instructions for the 'team' to arrive at the *Le Lac Leman* hotel on Sunday, the 16th of March. Reservations had been made for each person for that Sunday night, with Mario having booked for three nights, commencing the preceding Friday. On Sunday, Mario and Eddy would hire a boat to take them to the exploration vessel. From there, Mario would pick up the other three from the hotel using the *Senator Explorer*'s launch.

* * *

I had just gotten off the phone. As he promised he would, Max had called to tell me he had notified *New Scotland Yard* of the incident of the fraudulent money transfer. He had gone on to explain that he considered Herman was on the level, and his wife, while being questioned separately, had given him misleading information due to her being under a considerable amount of distress. He also informed the police that I had been instructed to carry out some discrete enquiries on behalf of the bank.

So, it seemed, I could expect a call, if not a visit from the police in the not too distant future.

I arrived home a little earlier than usual. I was going to make a return visit to one or both of the offices of 'Homes & Autos', but there was not enough time. I would make it my first job tomorrow.

As expected, upon my arrival at the office the following morning, there was a message already on the answering machine. Could I contact the police at the following number? I was told either I could visit them, or they could call on me if I would prefer. I opted for them to visit me at 2 pm after lunch that afternoon.

After a second cup of tea, I went about visiting both offices of 'Homes & Autos'; as expected, they were both still closed and with the same notices on the doors. I enquired at the neighbouring shops if anyone had been about or if they knew anything different since my last visit. Sadly, as I expected, I drew a blank.

Later that day, I told the police all I knew with regard to the Herman affair. I mentioned I had not been back long from checking the two insurance offices. With the little information I had given them, and what they'd gleaned from Max, they had a start. I told them not to hesitate to call me if they thought I could be of any further help.

*   *   *

It was Wednesday. Mario was in the final stages of packing what little he needed for his trip. He had to arrive in France ahead of the team in order to purchase certain items. The first requirement on his ever growing list was the double cell lithium battery-operated master key unit, after Ian Brown had told him a few days earlier it was now ready. The second requirement was the purchase of a bank; not a regular bank, but an address with a registered title where funds and mail could be received and sent. This he would complete after the coming exercise, as it was not an urgent requirement.

Mario had pre-booked a seat on the *Rail Europe* overnight train from London St. Pancras, direct to Lyon. It was no cheaper than flying, but much more comfortable, easier, and convenient.

He had arrived at St. Pancras a little after 8pm. While waiting to board the overnighter, he decided to purchase a takeaway snack for later (cheaper than on the train), as well as one for the morning when he arrived in France.

With still almost half an hour to kill, Mario went in search of the bar and a pint of ale.

As was guaranteed by *Rail Europe*, the train departed on time.

It was 9.30pm when Mario had his supper snack. It was not a lot, but he didn't need much, as he'd purposely had a good-sized lunch. He would have a nightcap in the train's bar before retiring to his sleeper berth.

It was 5:10am when the train pulled into *Lyon Part Dieu* railway station, four hundred and ninety-five miles south of London.

Mario took his time leaving the train; after all, he was in no hurry.

He found a taxi outside of the railway station and offered instructions to the driver to take him to one of the reliable car rentals in the area, open 24/7. Once in his Peugeot 405, he went in search of one of the many restaurants in Lyon that opened early.

Where Paris was famous for its superb architecture, Lyon was noted for its superb restaurants. This was not Mario's first time in Lyon, and it would probably not be his last.

He found a small café, *Le Monde,* and enjoyed a set breakfast menu of Café ou' the chocolat, Jus D'orange, Croissants and Pain Beurre Confiture, declared by the waiter to be a 'petite breakfast'. Mario reminded himself that this was France; everything was petite.

Although it was still early spring, the sun was well above the horizon when Mario left the café. He headed out of Lyon and for the D383, which would eventually take him to the A42.

The more he drove, the more the countryside took on a lush green appearance. Now well into March, and a few miles south of England, the weather was a good deal warmer; this suited Mario, as he was not a lover of the cold. Skiing holidays in Switzerland and France were at the bottom of his list. In the English winter, the Canary Islands were near the top.

Unable to check-in to his hotel before 1pm, Mario took his time driving. With a pleasant day and beautiful countryside, there was no hurry.

When Mario did eventually arrive at the *Le Lac Leman*, he was surprised at how quiet it was. Of course, it was early in the year, even though it was the start to the weekend.

Built mostly of stone, the four star *Le Lac Leman* was in its earlier days a splendid chateau; now it was transformed into a small thirty-six room hotel. The rear of the hotel faced onto the shores of *Lake Geneva*. It had a private one hundred meter wooden pier with fishing and boating facilities. Although it boasted only thirty-six guest rooms, it was well renowned for the fine food in its two restaurants, open to non-residents as well as residents. The hotel also had an indoor pool and a fitness centre.

Mario was not interested in any of these, at least not at the moment. He was, however, interested in the restaurants. The only thing that stopped the *Le Lac Leman* from being a five star hotel was the fact that its location was a little remote and it had no lifts, being only three stories.

On arrival, one was set back a hundred years by the architecture of the interior. A magnificent sweeping spiral staircase took guests to their suites on the first and second floors. Also, the carvings of ancient animals on the upper sections of the reception area and public rooms were most vivid in their portrayal.

Mario checked-in and was given directions to his room on the first floor. After unpacking, he laid out a change of clothes before taking a shower, then lay on the bed for a brief moment before dressing and going down to the lunch restaurant. Having had a light supper the evening before, and an equally light early breakfast, Mario was feeling a little peckish.

After an enjoyable lunch of pork cutlets, potato Dauphinoise and fresh French beans, Mario returned to his room. Checking his list of things to do before Sunday, he decided first he would visit a previous acquaintance who could supply him with liquid concentrate of ferric chloride; this he needed as a back-up in case the rechargeable electronic deposit box master key system didn't work. Unfortunately, it had already been established that there was no way of prior checking. Mario had asked Ian Brown what the success rate was, and Ian had replied between eighty and ninety-five percent.

* * *

Ferric chloride came in two forms, powder or liquid. Both were safe until coming in contact with water. The liquid form came in dropper bottle packs and was concentrated and three times more powerful; for obvious reasons, that was the form Mario needed.

Mario picked up his car and room key from the coffee table and went down to reception. Leaving his room key in the key deposit box, he gave the car key to the attendant at the main entrance to bring his rental car around.

* * *

A week had passed since my last meeting with Walter Prendigast. I had not heard from Walter, and neither had Henry, as he had promised during our last meeting.

Likewise, I had not heard from the police with regard to the mysterious loan of £4million. It had been agreed that I would bill Max Hoffer for work carried out so far, as the police were now covering the investigation.

I telephoned Henry for advice on what he thought was the best next move regarding the Parkinson affair.

"Henry," I said once I was connected, "I'm not too happy with the Parkinson affair. Prendigast was really agitated over the possibility that a serious crime might have been committed. What do you suggest is our next move— if any?"

"Well, Brian me boy, I would maybe wait a little longer, particularly as the Kirby factory has now closed. This could well be taking up any spare time Walter Prendigast might have. If we don't hear from him in the next couple of days, one of us can give him a call to see what he has to say, and we can take it from there."

"Sounds reasonable," I told Henry. At that point, I hung up.

*   *   *

Mario drove back the way he had come to arrive back at the town centre of Yvoire. Glancing at the paper on the passenger seat next to him, he followed the directions given. He eventually arrived at the chemical warehouse. He had been told that when he arrived, he should telephone, then someone would be there to let him in. Mario was a little uncertain as to the need for such security. The establishment was quite legal, but more and more places were adopting this line of approach as a security measure, chemical warehouses and gun shops in particular.

Sure enough, within a few minutes of his call, he saw the shutter rise and someone unlock the door. Mario stepped into the shop and shook hands with a gentleman who introduced himself as Maurice. The premises were smaller than Mario had expected—that was, until he was shown to the rear of the building. There, the place opened up to a much larger area. There was everything from forty-five gallon drums of boiler chemical treatment to cases of two-hundred-and-fifty ml bottles of swimming pool chemicals, both for testing and treatment, and trays of even smaller quantities.

The product Mario was interested in came in small trays of a dozen 50ml drip bottles per tray. Each bottle would do two to three deposit boxes.

Maurice enquired as to how much ferric chloride Mario wanted.

"Five trays," Mario told him.

Five was more than he needed, but he wanted to be sure he had enough, just in case.

"Delivery?"

Mario gave him the necessary information, paid, then took his leave.

There was not enough time left to do any more 'shopping', so Mario decided to return to the hotel.

On his arrival back at the hotel, he noted there were a couple of hours before dinner. Having had a late lunch, Mario decided on a late dinner, then decided after all to have a swim in the heated indoor pool; this he thought would help his appetite for dinner.

After his swim, which Mario had to admit he rather enjoyed, he showered, took a brief rest before dressing, then went down to the reception. The idea was to catch up on any local news; never a bad thing when you're away from home.

At 8:00pm, Mario entered the restaurant and found a discreet table near the window, which he was informed had an excellent view of the garden and the setting sun before darkness had fallen.

As Mario anticipated, choosing the evening meal would be the most difficult part of the day. He narrowed the choice down to filet steak, asparagus and creamed potatoes with a mushroom sauce, or Mediterranean sword fish steak, grilled tomatoes and sauterne potatoes. Then it dawned on him, the solution was simple: whichever one he didn't have tonight, he would have tomorrow. Sunday evening, he would possibly eat in town—problem solved.

After an enjoyable dinner, Mario returned to the reading area of the lounge bar, ordered a cognac and read the highlights of the last couple of days in a copy of the English *Daily Mail*.

Tomorrow, he hoped he would finish his shopping. He needed certain items from various places. At the supermarket he would get a supply of food for five persons, enough to last a couple of weeks, and at the marina he would get oxygen bottles and fuel for the *Senator Explorer*, all to be delivered directly to the vessel.

* * *

It was mid-morning. I was in my office, pondering what to do next, when the phone rang.

"Good morning, Mr. Ridley," a female voice said. "Please wait a moment."

A few seconds later, Max Hoffer came on the line.

CHAPTER 10

IT WAS RAINING, A LIGHT drizzle, when Mario left the hotel to complete his shopping. The forecast was that the rain would not last long. Among other things on his list were heavy duty black polythene garbage bags from the hardware store. These would be used to load the contents of the depository deposit boxes before being transported by the submersible back to the *Senator Explorer.* Mario considered he would have a full day.

On his return to the hotel, as he collected his room key, he was informed there was a message for him. It read rather like a 1950s British telegram: 'Be advised I am on the way, EG' was all it said. *Good*, Mario thought. He was ready and more than happy with what he had achieved during the day and the way things were going so far.

After his second shower of the day, Mario went to the bar for a pre-dinner drink. It was quiet in the bar, as well as the restaurant, but it was certain to get busy by the coming holiday weekend.

*　*　*

"Yes?" I said, picking up the phone.

"I need to speak to Mr. Ridley, please."

"Speaking," I replied into the mouthpiece.

"This is Max Hoffer," he said.

I didn't like to say that I'd recognised the voice.

"Yes, Max. Good to hear from you," I replied.

"You won't believe it," he almost shouted.

"What?" I enquired.

"The bank has just received half a million GB pounds as a first payment on the four million pound loan of a little over three months ago."

"Actually, Max, I'm not too surprised. I always thought there was something genuine about the guy who forced Herman to grant the loan in the first place."

"Why do you say that?" Max asked.

"Basically, because there was very little violence. No bullets in the gun, no bomb – nothing!"

"Yes, but why?"

"I think our friend is on some sort of a mission. Don't ask me what, when, where, or why, but I had this feeling almost from the start, a mission that he prefers should suffer no casualties."

"Well, that's why one of our solicitors, Henry, suggested you for this job. He said you had good instincts."

"So what would you like me to do now?" I asked.

"If it's at all possible, keep your eyes open and ears to the ground. I think if you're right, then our friend picked this bank for a reason. This could be our first real lead."

"A very good point, Max," I replied.

*   *   *

Mario sat down for the second evening in the dinner restaurant and ordered the swordfish steak. His second evening would be similar to his first by way of unwinding after a long day and an enjoyable meal. One thing he had to do before retiring was check over everything and ensure he had not forgotten anything or made any mistakes.

Once in the lounge bar with a cognac and this time the local English language newspaper, Mario checked the latest news before going about more serious business.

Having read the parts of the paper that interested him, he ordered a second cognac before getting down to checking every last detail in his notes and in his diary, some of which were coded.

There had been no indication in the message he had been given by the hotel receptionist as to when the other members of the team would be arriving. That did not matter after all; he had given them individual instructions, as they had not met each other.

The following morning after breakfast, Mario returned to the town. There was one last job he needed to do. He would return to the hotel for a light lunch, catch up on the latest daily paper while letting his lunch settle, then rest for an hour before enjoying another swim in the indoor pool, a half hour workout, and shower before the cocktail hour—two for the price of one.

*   *   *

Max Hoffer had notified the police that there had been a turn of events regarding the 'unauthorised loan' by way of the fact that half-a-million pounds had been repaid as was promised at the time of the four million GB pound transfer—but 'not' expected.

I told Max I would come down tomorrow and see if there was anything that could be learnt from the first repayment, as well as have a word with Herman on the issue. While visiting the bank, I would return the videotape to Max so he could pass it on to the police if he so desired.

Later, I telephoned Henry and brought him up to date. At the same time, I asked if he had heard from Walter Prendigast. He told me he had not.

What is he playing at? I wondered.

*   *   *

Eddy Grant arrived at the *Le Lac Leman* mid-afternoon. Mario had not yet returned from Yvoire.

Eddy checked into his pre-booked room, unpacked, and took a shower. After his shower and a change of clothes, he felt a lot better. He returned to the reception and enquired if a Mario Petri was in the hotel. The receptionist told Mr. Grant that he had not returned from an errand of earlier that morning.

"Would you be kind enough to tell him a Mr. Grant is waiting for him in the coffee lounge?"

"Most certainly, sir."

Eddy decided the best plan was for him to wait near the entrance of the coffee lounge so he could see Mario when he returned. He had not met Mario face-to-face but had a full description of what he looked like. While he waited, he ordered a cappuccino coffee.

He did not have long to wait.

He saw a fellow coming through the main entrance who looked very much like Mario Petri. The man went to the reception, presumably for his room key, and was given the message left by Eddy. This was obvious as he turned around immediately to see if he recognised anyone, enquiring at the same time where the coffee lounge was.

Mario came over to Eddy, who was now standing.

"Good to meet you," Eddy said.

"Likewise," Mario returned. "I'll be eating in the hotel restaurant around seven if you would care to join me." He had decided not to have dinner in town; the food was excellent at the hotel.

"Love to. In the meantime, join me in a coffee."

At dinner, Mario told Eddy that after breakfast they would take the boat over to the *Senator Explorer*.

"We won't take the hotel boat, as it has a set routine," Mario said. "Instead, we'll get the boat from Yvoire; I don't want any connections between us here at the hotel and the *Senator Explorer*."

"What time do you intend to have breakfast?" Eddy asked.

"No hurry; around nine."

*   *   *

I had received a call from the police bringing me up to date on the Goldsworth affair. I didn't like to mention that the president of the bank had already brought me up to date on the matter; however, I did repeat my offer to help if needed. What they did say was that the two insurance offices trading under the name of 'Homes and Autos' were now let to two other firms: one a solicitor, the other a deli specializing in a variety of hams and cheeses.

I was tempted to take a look, then decided against the idea. I considered that there was nothing to be gained, at least not at this point in time.

Neither Henry nor I had heard from Walter. While I was contemplating the issue, the phone rang.

"Brian?"

"Yes," I answered.

"It's Henry."

"How are you?" I asked.

"I'm fine, Brian, and yourself?"

"Yes, likewise, I'm fine."

"I need to let you know that Walter has disappeared from the planet. No report was made to the tax people in Caxton, so we're considering him the number one suspect in our investigation as to whether or not there's any foul play at Parkinson's."

"Did he resign, or maybe he's off sick?"

"Not sure at the moment. I telephoned Walter for an update on the situation at hand and was informed he wasn't available, but I'll keep you posted."

"Thanks, Henry," I said. "Call me if you need anything." I then finished the call.

*   *   *

Mario arrived at the breakfast hall a fraction after nine. Eddy Grant was already sitting at a table near the window with a view over the lake.

"Good morning. Mind if I join you?"

"No, not at all. Please do."

Seeing a new customer enter the dining room for breakfast, a waiter came over and offered Mario a choice of tea or coffee, at the same time offering the a-la-carte menu.

"Coffee, please," he informed the waiter, refusing the a-la-carte menu.

While Mario waited for his coffee, he went to browse the breakfast buffet selection. There was live cooking for a variety of eggs, as well as bacon. At the buffet counter, amongst other things, there were mushrooms, tomatoes, and onion, all of which could be taken over to the live cooking station, as well as ham, sliced fried potatoes, and other choices. Mario plumed for two fried eggs, taking over a plate of mushroom and tomatoes for cooking. He then returned for a helping of fried potatoes and a slice of ham.

After breakfast, he enjoyed a second coffee in the coffee lounge while Eddy went up to pack the few items he had unpacked. Mario had already packed and left his bag with the concierge on the way down to breakfast. While Mario waited for Eddy, he looked at the local English language paper to check the latest news; there was nothing of any importance.

When Mario saw Eddy return to reception, he placed the paper back on the rack and joined him at check-out.

At the front entrance to the hotel, Mario got a taxi. There were always two or three outside waiting for a fare.

"Yvoire boat pier, please," Mario instructed the driver.

CHAPTER 11

MARIO HAD RENTED A BOAT to take them to the *Senator Explorer*. By the time they arrived, the sun was high in the sky.

Two deliveries to the *Senator Explorer* were expected later that morning. One was diesel fuel, the other was the food supplies, enough to last at least until they had completed their task, maybe a little extra. Along with the food supplies was this evening's prepared dinner; Mario's thinking was that there would be no time to cook an evening meal on their first day. While Mario checked the deliveries, Eddy checked over the *Senator Explorer's* tender, ready for collecting the rest of the team from the hotel the following day.

*   *   *

There was a low mist lying over the lake the following morning when Mario went up on deck, not unusual for the time of the year and being surrounded by so much water. Once the sun had been up a while, it would burn off the mist.

Eddy was on the bridge, checking over the instrumentation. Mario tapped on the bridge access door, and Eddy beckoned him in.

"Everything okay?" Mario asked.

"Seems to be, and most certainly will be by the time we're ready to move from here, that's for sure."

After breakfast and a coffee in the smoke room, Mario suggested they collect the other members of the team. The tender was tied up alongside the *Senator Explorer* by the steps down to the waterline.

Ian Brown, Nick Burrows and Collin Write were waiting in the hotel reception when Mario and Eddy arrived mid-morning. They had made each other's acquaintances by descriptions that had been passed around. Mario, not having met Collin Write, introduced himself. Collin was a stocky man—around 220 pounds, Mario guessed. He carried a pleasant smile, with light brown hair combed back from his forehead. He was wearing dark jeans and a cream seaman's style polar neck jumper.

It would seem everyone had met each other and become acquainted.

"Are we ready to proceed?" Mario asked.

There were nods and grunts all around.

It was late morning when they arrived at the vessel. As expected, the mist had cleared.

"We'll have a bite to eat for lunch, after which Ian, Nick and Collin can unpack, then get acquainted with the vessel. Eddy can check over the submersible and start charging the batteries, while I check the research room. After dinner, we can go over the plans in detail. Is that okay with everyone?"

Echoes of "Yes" sounded all around.

*   *   *

The cutting tool that had replaced the nose cone of the submersible looked very formidable indeed, taking up almost the entire front section of the submersible. It was quite heavy, counter balanced only by the two large set of batteries at the rear. It consisted of three rotating, forward tungsten carbide cutting tools angled at 35 degrees for ease of penetration. The tools rotated at variable speeds both clockwise and anticlockwise within the head, both controlled by the operator. The natural vibration of the cutting tool greatly assisted the penetration of what was being drilled. Centre to the boring tool was a two-and-a-half inch diameter rotary drill; this not only 'centered' the cutting cone, but also allowed for slow flooding of the depository while the larger hole was being cut.

Each set of the rear mounted batteries consisted of ten times twenty-four volt 'lifepo4' cells weighing a total of 210 kg. Going from flat to fully charged would take two-and-a-half hours; ultimately, the lifespan of the batteries depended on how the sub was operated.

Mario delivered the double key unlocking equipment, along with the ferric-chloride, to Eddy Grant at the sub.

"How is everything?" Mario asked.

"Everything seems okay. I'm charging both sets of batteries now, ready for tomorrow's test runs."

"How long for charging the batteries?" Mario asked.

"A little under three hours each set, I think," Eddy replied. "But we're able to charge both sets at the same time."

"Okay, I'll leave you to it, then."

Mario walked back to the control room. He had a collection of catalogues covering Russian artifacts, rare stamps and coins, and selected jewelry missing from the period 1941–1945; in fact, he had information on just about everything. He considered that he had not overlooked anything. He'd had many months to plan the operation. He would make one final check while there was still time.

*   *   *

I was sitting in my office, and a client was sitting opposite me when the phone rang.

"Hello, Henry," I said, seeing his name on the information panel. I held up my hand to indicate to the gentleman opposite me that I would only be a moment.

"Hello, Brian. I have some rather disturbing news."

"Oh, Henry, what may that be?"

"The Parkinsons' deputy director phoned me to tell me they were concerned about the absence of Walter Prendigast at the plant. They had phoned his house; however, there was no reply. Being further troubled, they sent one of the junior managers to his house. He couldn't gain access, so they then called the police."

"How did the Parkinsons know to call you?" I asked.

"Apparently, there was information in his office indicating he was in touch with us. At the moment, I'm not sure what that information was."

"Well, that doesn't really concern us."

"Correct, but what does concern us is, when the police finally gained access to the house, they found that he was dead, slouched in a chair. An empty glass and a nearly empty bottle of Kentucky Bourbon were on the coffee table beside him."

"So where do we go from here?" I asked Henry.

"We wait," Henry replied. "We're off the case regarding Walter. Let's see what happens over the next couple of days. I might add, the police at the moment aren't ruling out foul play."

"I'll wait until I hear from you then, Henry."

*   *   *

Mario had gathered his team in the smoke room of the *Senator Explorer,* a plan of the Brent Depository spread out on the table.

"The plan is," Mario said, "we have the next two days to go over everything thoroughly. We'll take the *Senator Explorer* up the lake in a northeasterly direction tomorrow, checking that everything is okay with her. At the same time, we'll try out the *FNRS* submersible, in order to get familiar with both. The following day, we'll return to the position we're at now. Thursday, we'll have most of the day to fully charge the submersible batteries. At approximately 5:30pm, Eddy and I will take the submersible to the lakeside wall of the Brent depository and drill a two-and-a-half inch hole into the depository's outer wall." Mario tapped the point marked on the plan.

"For what reason?" Eddy asked.

"Simply to flood the depository slowly," Mario replied. "It's been calculated that the inflow of water through a two-and-a-half inch hole six feet below the level of the lake will take four hours to flood the eight hundred and thirty-four cubic meters of the depository below the waterline. That's given the known water pressure of the lake at six feet below the surface. This will allow the air being replaced by water to escape at a slower rate, and therefore undetected. Any other questions so far?"

There were none.

Mario continued. "Once the small hole has been drilled, we'll return to the *Senator Explorer,* and I'll be replaced by Ian. Thereafter, you'll be in two two-man teams, Ian with Eddy, and Nick with Collin, who has similar experience as Eddy regarding submersibles. Again, any questions?"

Everybody looked at each other and shook their heads.

"Good. Is there anything anyone has a problem with?"

Again, no.

"Right oh. There are drinks in the mini bar. After tonight, there will be no alcohol until the operation is completed, after which there will be plenty."

*   *   *

Four days after receiving the news from Henry regarding the shameful death of Walter Prendigast, I got a call.

"Brian Ridley?"

"Yes," I said.

"Be careful."

"Who is this?" I asked.

"You need not worry about who this is; I'm a friend of yours *and* was of Walters. The autopsy on Mr. Prendigast showed traces of arsenic in his body. This, coupled with the consumption of three-quarters of a bottle of bourbon and high blood pressure, resulted in his death—which indicates trouble in the Parkinson camp. Whoever administered the poison seemingly knew Walter had a heart condition. Henry has been notified. I tell you this information, as it's certain there's foul play here, and your names could be on their list. Goodbye, Mr. Ridley."

The line went dead. I immediately called Henry.

"Yes," he said when I explained the reason for my call, "I had a similar call. We record all incoming calls. Security, you understand."

"Yes, a good idea. I appreciate that," I said. "I think maybe I should do the same."

"Wouldn't be such a bad idea, Brian."

*   *   *

Ten o'clock Tuesday morning, Mario weighed anchor and set a course for 7'E-48'N, at a modest speed of 16 knots. There was a maximum speed limit on the lake, of which Mario was not quite certain; seeing the speed of other craft on the lake, though, he was certain he was well below the maximum.

In the early afternoon, Mario had arrived at the point where he wanted to be. The depth sounder indicated it was okay to drop anchor.

"Eddy, you and Ian take the submersible first on a trial run. When you're both secured inside, Collin and Nick will winch you over the side. When you're semi-buoyant, they'll operate the quick release mechanism. I'll be in the control room for any communications."

"Sounds fine," Eddy replied, and then proceeded to the sub, with Nick following close behind.

Mario was in the control room when Eddy called in.

"So far, everything seems good," Eddy's voice crackled over the intercom.

"Good to know," Mario replied. "Give her a good workout. We don't want any problems when we start the exercise."

Almost two hours later, Eddy and Ian returned to the *Senator Explorer*. Mario went to greet them as they stepped out of the sub.

"How was everything?" he asked.

"Fine, no problems at all," Eddy replied. "Everything's working well."

"Good. Tomorrow morning, Collin and Nick can take the sub out so they can also get familiar with it. I'll let them know at dinner."

Mid-morning Wednesday, Collin and Nick were in the sub, being lowered into the water for them to carry out a couple of hour's familiarization. After lunch, Mario would up anchor and return to their original position not far from the hotel *Le Lac Leman*.

Activity on the lake had been quiet during the week, but Mario expected that would change at the holiday weekend, especially as the weather was expected to be good.

Thursday, back where they were in the earlier part of the week, Mario suggested everyone have a quiet day relaxing in preparation for the coming evening and weekend.

At exactly 5:30pm Thursday evening, Mario left with Eddy in the submersible to cross 'under' the border to Switzerland and the Brent depository. On their arrival at the Brent depository lakeside wall, Mario pointed to a point midway between two pillars and three meters above the base of the wall, approximately six feet below the surface. That was the point where the two-and-a-half inch hole should be drilled. The hole would act as a centre point for drilling the main entry hole later.

*   *   *

I had not long returned to my office after making certain enquiries on behalf of a new client. Max Hoffer called to see if I had managed to learn anything from the bank records of the loan to Mario Petri. I explained that I hadn't and had contacted an accountant friend of mine to see if he could decipher the documents. I assured Max that the person in question was above reproach and everything would be handled in the strictest of confidence; Max was more than happy with that.

Later in the day, Henry had called to see if I had heard any more regarding Walter Prendigast.

"Not a word," I told Henry. "Having looked closely at the company's public records, it would appear everything was above board."

"Well, it would also seem there's a possibility that Walter did in fact commit suicide. Taking the poison himself, and then downing almost a whole bottle of bourbon to ease any suffering."

"Why would he do that if everything was normal at the Parkinsons'?"

"That, Brian me boy, is the $64,000 question."

"Was he married?" I asked.

"I'm not sure, but I'll find out," Henry replied.

With that, I ended the call.

CHAPTER 12

AFTER DRILLING THE TWO-AND-A-HALF INCH hole, Eddy and Mario returned to the *Senator Explorer*. Ian changed over with Mario, and the batteries on the *FNRS* were recharged, as the main drilling operation would need fully charged batteries, then the sub would return to the depository.

Now Friday, it was a little after midnight when the speaker in the control room crackled and Eddy reported they had broken through.

"Good, well done. Return to the *Senator Explorer*. We'll recharge the batteries, by which time Collin and Nick can relieve you," Mario replied.

It was still dark on the surface of the lake on Friday morning when the sub returned to the depository. Mario had used the time to catch up on a little sleep himself, and he was now fully awake and standing by in the control room.

The time it would take between each trip was governed by the length of time the oxygen tanks lasted, rather than how much they could carry back to the mother ship each time. This was considered to be seventy-five minutes maximum, as they would be exerting a considerable amount of energy most of the time.

Mario looked at his watch; it was 7:00am when Nick informed Mario they were on their way back.

So far, everything was looking good; everything was going according to plan—and more importantly, on time.

Mario would wait until the sub had returned, unloaded its 'cargo', and recharged the batteries before calling Eddy and Ian, allowing them time to have something to eat before departing. While Eddy and Ian were on the 'second run', Mario would start to catalogue, where possible, the items that had been gathered so far.

*   *   *

While having lunch with Henry the day before, I had informed him I'd taken the liberty of sending the information on the Goldsworth Bank's forced loan to the Mr. person unknown to an accountant I knew to be reliable and had informed Max Hoffer, with his approval. I also sought Henry's advice on doing the same regarding the Parkinson's affair. Parkinson's had gone public two years ago, but the Parkinson family controlled forty percent of the company; this meant the accounts were available for scrutiny not just by shareholders, but anybody.

"Why not?" he said. "It can't do any harm."

I agreed.

*   *   *

Mario was still in the control room when the intercom came alive. It was almost mid-day.

"We're on our way back," Eddy's voice announced.

"All right," Mario replied. "We're standing by. Everything okay?"

"Yes, everything's good."

Mario was very pleased with the first 'delivery' and calculated by the number of boxes already opened that he was still on schedule—both in time and value. The larger boxes may take a little longer, as he suspected this was where the gold ingots would be. So far, only one box had proved difficult to open with the waterproof 'electronic key', and the concentrated ferric chloride had been used with considerable success.

By now, Mario had only had time to catalogue and estimate half of the 'first delivery'. So far, so good, he considered, but now was not the time to be complacent.

Again, Collin and Nick would relieve Eddy and Ian once the sub was ready to return for the third trip.

Mario decided to call a pause on the return trip to the depository while the batteries were recharging, in order to have the chance for an early dinner together. This would give everyone an opportunity to exchange any information.

After dinner, Collin and Nick returned to the Brent depository. Meanwhile, Mario continued to evaluate the 'gains' so far, while Eddy and Ian rested.

For the next two days, the 'teams' continued with their steady alternating routine. As Mario had expected, some of the larger boxes contained various gold ingots, from 1oz to 1kg (depending on the country of origin), as well as a number of paintings in sealed tubes.

By Easter Monday morning, they had completed their task and were ready to leave the area and return to the original position where they had tested the submersible.

Mario wanted to put as much distance between the *Senator Explorer* and the Brent depository as possible. Tuesday morning, the depository staff would discover the flooding when they could not open the massive access door due to the system's interlocking safety system. Divers would be sent down to investigate, where they would discover the two-and-a-half foot diameter hole and realize an underwater vessel of some sort had been employed. Without a doubt, this would result in a dragnet of the entire lake.

The second half of Mario's plan was to put the 'haul' into the many black, heavy, duty double skinned bags he had purchased on his second day in France, as soon as possible. Once at his new location, he would pay the four crew members a further ten percent of their agreed monies and send them ashore with the *Senator Explorer's* tender for a mini break. He told them they would get the rest of the money once they left the *Senator Explorer* for the final time before going their separate ways. While they were ashore, Mario would up anchor and move to a new position where the bottom of the lake was only one hundred and forty meters below the hull of the vessel. At this point, he would 'drop' the black bags containing the items from the depository. He made a note of the exact latitude and longitude by marking the position on the chart with a prick from the point of the chartroom compass, thereby giving nothing away to prying eyes. He—and only he—would know the point at which the bags had been dropped. He would then return to his original position, ready for the return of his men. Nobody except Mario would know where the treasure was.

*   *   *

I had just returned to the office when I received a telephone call from my accountant friend, Bernard.

"Brian Ridley?" the voice asked.

"Speaking," I replied.

"I've looked at the Parkinson accounts, and I'm sorry to say there are discrepancies in the figures. It would appear there have been changes made from the original accounts, something only a qualified accountant could do—or would find."

"What exactly are you saying?" I enquired.

"I think you need to come over. I can explain better person to person."

"When will be convenient?" I asked.

"Whenever you like," came the reply.

"How about now?"

"Yes, if you like. I'm here for the rest of the day."

Before leaving the office, I called Henry; he was out, and his secretary informed me he should be back within the hour.

I gave Henry's secretary a message, asking if he could call me back when he returned. This, she said she would do.

*   *   *

It was a little after breakfast when Mario and the team weighed anchor and headed northeast, keeping on the French side of the border.

Mario called Eddy to the control room.

"Once we're underway, I'd like you and the team to remove the cutting head from the sub, then replace it with the original nose cone. I've set a course with the autopilot for a point midway between Lausanne and Evian, which is the deepest part of the lake, about three hundred and ten meters deep. There, we'll 'loose' the cutting tool."

"Well, that's quite deep," Eddy replied. "Considering the total area of the lake, I guess it'll take some finding, if ever."

Mario continued. "Then after that, we'll go to the position where we tested the sub a week ago. You and the others can have the rest of the day ashore, a few drinks, and a good meal, but you must return before midnight. I'll give you a further advance on your monies; the rest you'll receive before we all go our separate ways."

"That sounds good," Eddy replied. "I'll tell the others."

* * *

When I returned to the office after meeting with Bernard, there was a message on my answering machine; it was Henry returning my call. I made a cup of tea, sat down at my desk, and called Henry back.

"Hello," Henry said. "My secretary said you'd called earlier."

"Yes, Henry. My accountant friend I was telling you about called me earlier. He said he felt certain the accounts of Parkinson's had been 'tampered' with. In fact, I've just come back from a visit with him. He gave me a broad outline of the situation, but I really need your advice on our next move."

"Maybe I can meet this accountant friend of yours."

"I think that would be a good idea."

* * *

Mario saw the crew out of sight, then weighed anchor. Although the *Senator Explorer* was far from new, she had been well maintained. She had been kept up to date and was well equipped, therefore easy to operate single-handedly. It only took Mario a little over an hour to arrive at the spot where he would disembark his cargo. He had put most of the items into small bags to make them easier to handle. It didn't take long before Mario was back at the position he occupied earlier, a little less than three hours ago.

It was now a good time for an early dinner, as this evening he was eating on his own. Mario went to the galley freezer and selected a filet of beef steak. It would be a simple meal this evening, but an enjoyable one nonetheless. Steak, egg, French fries with fried mushrooms and grilled sun dried Mediterranean tomatoes—his favorite.

After dinner, Mario went on deck to double check that there was no trace of anything to indicate the submersible had been used for anything other than the survey of the bed of the lake. Satisfied all was well, he then went to the control room to check for the same. He had buried his brochures along with the takings from the Brent depository a little over a couple of hours ago.

Mario would wait up until the return of his crew.

It was 11:10pm when the crew returned to the *Senator Explorer,* slightly the worse for wear.

Mario informed the men they would stay on board for two or three more days. He said he would explain in the morning.

At the start of breakfast, Mario explained his reasoning for wishing to delay their departure and not wanting to be in too much of a hurry to leave the area.

"We need to be around and working when one of the patrol boats eventually catches up with us. Several months ago," Mario continued, "while I was researching the Brent

Depository, I also researched the loss of a particular ferry during the tail end of the Second World War. It was the *Morning Mist,* one of the historic *Belle Époque* paddle steamer ferry boats that frequented the lake during the early and mid 1940s. She was believed to have sunk between Evian in France and Lausanne in Switzerland while transporting gold and other artifacts out of Germany."

Eddy Grant was the first to break into Mario's speech.

"What are you saying, Mario? Has the wreck never been found?"

"That's precisely the case. You see, she left Evian but never arrived at Lausanne. One reason is that it was believed a bomb was planted aboard the ferry, set to explode when the ferry was halfway into her voyage. Unfortunately, the ferry was late leaving Lausanne. I have now discovered just how late, one-and-a-half hours to be precise. This gives us a better picture of just where she's sitting on the bottom of the lake, one-and-a-half hours short of halfway."

"How deep?" Ian Brown asked.

"About two-hundred-and-ten meters," Mario replied. "That is, if my calculations of her position and the information about her time of departure are correct. We're talking on the French side of the border. I would point out that if anything is discovered, it is a bonus to be shared between the five of us, and no one else—less my additional expenses, of course."

"That sounds fair," Nick Burrows announced.

"We'll depart for that area after breakfast and there's no longer a time table to work to."

*   *   *

Henry and I had arranged to meet up with Bernard at his house this coming afternoon, as he worked from home, being self-employed. I had given Henry directions on how to get there, and I arrived at Bernard's house a fraction early so as to be there when Henry arrived.

As always, Henry was on time. Bernard asked if we would like a drink of any kind. I settled for a glass of orange juice, while Henry had soda-water.

"First, may I tell you there's nothing suspicious about the contract for the four million loan from the Goldsworth Bank. It's a standard contract; however, regarding the Parkinson accounts, there's been some skillful book keeping," Bernard remarked after we were seated around his dining table. "It would also appear that it wasn't the work of one person," he continued. "For example, the amount spent on R&D is not conducive with the company's product or turnover. Likewise, the amount showing supposedly spent on security is far too high. Transport is another factor. With the younger brother locked away, the only private transport was the elder brother's *Rolls Royce*. With the Kirby factory now closed, there are fewer company vehicles than before, and those are on lease, mostly at Caxton. So you see, the deductions are, again, much too high."

"So what you're saying," Henry broke in, "is that the accounts here are not a true copy of the original accounts?"

"That about sums it up," Bernard replied.

"What do you think we should do?" I asked Bernard.

"A good question," he replied. "I don't know if I'm the best person to answer it, though. I believe, Brian, you said your client is no longer with us. That makes it a little bit tricky."

"I appreciate what you're saying, Bernard, but our then client paid us a retainer, so we feel obliged to see it through, at least as far as possible."

"Okay, here's what *I* would do in a similar situation. First, I'd take a copy of these accounts to the regional Inland Revenue office in Caxton and explain the situation to them. They can refer to me if you wish. Then I'd go to the police investigating the death of your client and bring them up to date on any progress on your side, then walk away! I'm sure by doing that, you'll have more than fulfilled your obligation."

CHAPTER 13

MARIO HAD MADE AN ACCURATE list of the items from the Brent Depository. He posted the list to his home address in Bedfordshire, along with photos, where necessary. He would get accurate valuations before returning to Lake Geneva. Should the list go astray, it would not damage his plans, only delay them, as the items were technically no longer existent.

He was pondering this and other issues while at the same time consulting a chart of the lake, in the area where they were. It was at this point where the *Morning Mist* was believed to have sunk while transporting the ill-gotten artifacts from Germany through France, to finally end up in Switzerland. Eddy Grant and Nick Burrows were out in the submersible, blowing sand at the bottom of the lake in the hopes of uncovering any possible treasure or evidence of any wreck. They would be back soon. Collin Write was checking over the generator and dipping the port and starboard fuel tanks. Ian Brown was checking over the crane while waiting for the submersible to return.

Ian came hurrying to the chart room at the rear of the bridge.

"It looks like there's an official boat heading directly towards us," he told Mario.

"Okay, then, let's go see."

Mario followed Ian onto the main deck. Sure enough, a boat some thirty feet plus in length and—by the size of the bow-wave—traveling at some considerable speed, was heading in their direction to the starboard side. More by reflex than anything else, Mario glanced at the mast and noticed they were flying the French flag.

The oncoming patrol boat was white, with *'#4 patrol'* on the side in large red letters.

Mario knew the French officials worked closely with the Swiss officials, and vice-versa.

"Ahoy there," a voice bellowed out through a megaphone as the patrol boat advanced on the *Senator Explorer*. "We need to come aboard and speak with the captain or the owner," the voice continued.

Mario waved his consent. He had not been underway; just drifting very slightly, while at the same time keeping a check on his position and recording the depth.

The patrol boat headed for their stern then made a last-minute sharp turn to starboard. As they were almost alongside, they threw a line to the *Senator Explorer,* an indication to secure the patrol boat alongside the *Senator Explorer*'s bows before throwing a second line to secure the stern.

"I'm Commander Laurent of the combined French and Swiss Customs and Lake Control," the officer said as he saluted and climbed aboard the *Senator Explorer*.

"I'm the owner of this vessel, the name is Mario Petri," Mario said, returning the salute. "What can I do for you?"

"We're looking for a vessel we suspect may be similar to this one," Commander Laurent replied.

"May I ask for what reason?" Mario enquired.

"An extremely serious bank depository break-in," Commander Laurent replied.

"Well, you're very much welcome to search the boat, Commander," Mario invited. "Take as long as you like. Take one of my men; he'll be able to assist you."

"How many of you are there in total?" the commander asked.

"Five," Mario said. "At the moment, two are on the submersible, surveying the bottom of the lake."

"What for, may I ask?"

"Our research indicates that in late 1944, one of the historic Belle Époque paddle steamers was sunk in this area while ferrying gold and other artifacts from Germany to Switzerland. What we don't know is how genuine the gold was. It was a known fact that during the last stages of the war, Germans were spraying iron bars with gold paint, throwing in a mixture of cheap artifacts and letting news leak out of the transportation of a valuable shipment. The idea was to lead the enemy into thinking it was the real thing. In the meantime, the genuine 'stuff' was being sneaked out the back door, so to speak."

"I take it you've been given authority in this area?" Commander Laurent asked.

"But of course," Mario replied. "I'll get the permit while you go with my man and search the ship. We have a plan layout of the vessel, if it'll help," Mario added.

*   *   *

I left the office early, as I had brought everything up to date. Tomorrow, I had a new assignment: a rather boring and monotonous job of surveillance. I would know more once I had met the client; nonetheless, it was a job that helped pay the bills.

I had left the final decision on how to handle the Parkinson affair with Henry. It seemed to me that any decision was more in Henry's line of work than mine—legal, rather than investigative. He had decided to act on Bernard's suggestion, first to the tax office in Caxton, after which I accompanied Henry to the police station, also in Caxton.

When I arrived home, Christina was in the garden brushing the last of the winter leaves off the lawn.

"Hello, my dear," I said, wrapping my arms around her shoulders.

"You're home early," she said while rubbing her hands down her pinafore.

"Yes," I replied. "I'm about up to date with everything, that is, until tomorrow. Then I start a new case, one I think will be fairly straightforward."

"Well, in that case, I'll finish up here and get the dinner underway."

"Take your time, my dear, there's no hurry," I replied.

Over dinner, I suggested to Christina that maybe I could take a week off from work while the weather was still cold and we could go somewhere warmer. My daughter Mary-Ann, from my first marriage, was now married with a teenage daughter and son of her own. My two daughters from my marriage with Christina were now also married; Angela was expecting their first baby soon. We didn't have to work around school holidays any more, and things were fairly quiet in the office at the moment, other than my possible new case tomorrow. One had to take advantage of opportunities.

"That's not a bad idea," she said while taking a sip of her drink. "I think we could both do with a break. It's been quite a while since our last break."

"Right, then. I'll see what my impending new client wants tomorrow, and we'll take it from there."

*　　*　　*

Collin Write was standing by, in readiness for the return of the sub. Mario had asked Ian if he would accompany the commander on a tour of the vessel. It was at this point the radio crackled.

"Hello, Mario, it's Eddy here. We think we've found a one kilo gold bar."

"Very interesting. It's important you mark the spot where you found it before leaving the site."

"Will do."

"Eddy, Collin and I will be standing by to see you back on board. Ian is giving a commander from one of the lake patrol boats a tour of our vessel, looking for possible stolen goods; however, come back as soon as your time is up."

"Right oh."

Mario went down to join Collin, in readiness for the return of the sub. He brought Collin up to date on events, including the finding of a possible gold bar. Mario had received word that the sub was on its way back. As the sub was being hoisted on board, Commander Laurent appeared with Ian.

"Everything seems to be in order," the commander said as he approached the area where the sub was being hoisted. Glancing at the submersible, Commander Laurent saw the vessel was no way capable of being used in connection with any depository or bank break-in.

"Glad to hear it," Mario replied. "Would you like to stay and join us over a spot of lunch?"

"No, thank you. We have much to do. Oh, by the way—again, what exactly is it you're doing here?"

"We believe a paddle steamer ferry sank in this area about fifty years ago, carrying German stolen loot to Switzerland, but her exact position was never really known, and it was never certain if the loot was genuine. Our aim is to answer both questions. Are you sure you won't stop for a spot of lunch?"

"Certain, but thank you."

Mario saw the commander off the boat, saluted, then returned to the sub.

"So, you think you two might have found a gold bar?" Mario said as they climbed aboard. "We'll, let's have some lunch I prepared earlier this morning—chicken salad, and tonight a curry with the remains of the chicken. While we have lunch, the sub's batteries can be charged, then Collin and Ian can take the sub back out and carry on where you two left off. While you're out on the sub, I'll test the gold bar and let you know the result as soon as I'm able."

"Sounds good to me," Ian said.

After lunch, Collin and Ian took the sub back to the point where Eddy had marked on the map. Eddy and Nick were taking a short nap before seeing to the return of the sub.

Mario was in the control room. In one corner was a selection of instruments for testing the purity of the gold.

Mario considered there was nothing suspicious about it being on board. He had already told the patrol boat commander what their purpose in the area was. He had also shown the commander the certificate issued by the French authorities.

The gold bar certainly weighed a kilo. One trick was to hollow out between thirty and thirty-five percent of a given size bar, then fill it with lead or any other soft metal with a similar weight as gold. Mario took the gold bar over to a small pillar drill fitted with a special drill that would extract a micro 'core' from the centre. This he would use to analyze the purity of the gold throughout the whole bar. Centering the gold bar, Mario started to drill. It did not take long; gold was a soft, non-ferrous metal. Retracting the drill, Mario released the one-mm thick core and noticed there was no change in color throughout its length; this was a good sign.

Mario was very careful in the handling of the miniature core so as not to break it, as it would have to be carefully replaced back into the gold bar. He carried out three tests that would define that first it *was* gold, and secondly its purity.

After Mario had completed his tests, he was satisfied that the gold was genuine. The only thing he was not sure about was the authenticity of its origin. Using his catalogue of 'World' Gold Refiners, he could find nothing with the markings on the bar in front of him. There was a trade mark, and below this was the country of origin, then 1K + Fine gold + 999.9, and finally the bar number and three stars. From the density test, it had been proven that the bar was the equivalent of 24K, which was all that really interested him. He didn't care if it was from 'back street' Germany, or anywhere else for that matter; gold was gold.

Mario gave his crew the good news over dinner, the chicken curry with Pelew rice that had been simmering for the last three hours, complete with side dishes of grated coconut, mango chuckney, slices of peeled cucumber and bananas, and a dried currant mix, complete with a serving of pompadoms.

"Today's value," Mario said, "for one kilo of 999.9 pure gold is something in the region of eight thousand pounds sterling. Divide that by five, and it works out at a fraction over sixteen hundred pounds each."

Nick let out a low whistle.

"I've made several tests, and I can assure you it's a genuine gold bar. The only thing I'm not sure of is its origin. That could detract from its value, but only very slightly."

"So what now?" Eddy enquired.

"Seeing as we have a few more days on our exploration license, and not wishing to arouse any suspicions by making a premature departure, I suggest we carry on 'treasure hunting'; it can only be to everyone's advantage.

CHAPTER 14

AS IT TURNED OUT, MY new client was in fact two clients! A husband and wife—a Mr. and Mrs. Henderson. Mr. Henderson owned a factory producing, among other things, computer security software, and some of the research was highly classified. It would appear their daughter had fallen in with a person of a seemingly unreliable character. The Henderson's were a little more than concerned, particularly in their line of business, as well as for the welfare of their daughter.

It had fallen upon me to make some discrete enquiries into the person of a Mr. Nigel Forester, apparently of half-Italian origin, working at a high class Italian restaurant by the name of *Lui-Phips,* on the outskirts of Northampton.

It had been decided that we meet at Mr. Henderson's factory. His office was spacious. One wall was a wall to wall window overlooking the Northampton football ground, home of the *cobblers*. A fine view if you liked football; I'm afraid I do not, but Mr. Henderson did. On the remaining three walls were a collection of various prints, including one of the football team of two years ago.

The floor was highly polished parquet. The central desk was glass topped. In front was a three-seater black soft leather settee.

Mr. Henderson wore a dark blue pinstriped cotton suit of obvious quality and a pale blue tie. He had almost ink black hair, swept back from his forehead.

I had told them I would get started right away and keep them informed on my findings, but I would be on a brief holiday for a few days in about a week's time. I assured them the necessary wheels would be set in motion prior to my departure. There didn't seem to be a problem with that.

On my return to the office, there was a message on the answering machine; it was Henry wanting to update me with the latest information on the Parkinson affair. I returned his call.

"I got your message," I told Henry when he picked up.

"Good afternoon, Brian. I thought I'd let you know the police in Caxton are treating the Parkinson affair as 'foul play'."

"Are they indeed?" I said. "Does that mean we're definitely no longer on the case?" I enquired.

"It does, me boy," he replied. "It would seem they're going to make a visit to Mr. Parkinson Jr."

"I thought they'd covered everything before he went to court, and eventually prison?" I said.

"Yes, but this time it isn't counterfeiting, but embezzlement! Not that Mr. P Jr. can be guilty this time, but he may be able to give the police some idea of who else *may* be guilty! He'll obviously try his hardest not to implicate his brother."

"It would be nice to be kept informed, though," I replied, "especially as we were involved from the very beginning. And I still don't understand why the purposely built factory in Kirby had to close down after only a few years in operation?"

"Maybe the police can find out. I'll have a word with them. How's everything else?" Henry asked.

I told him I had just gotten back from seeing a new client and briefly outlined the case. I also mentioned I would be away for a few days the day after tomorrow, a last-minute booking. Tomorrow, I would start my investigations on the new case.

"Have a pleasant trip. I'll see you when you get back."

*   *   *

Mario stayed at the site of the wreckage a further three days. In that time, they had managed to salvage a further four bars of gold, each one kilo in weight and identical to the first. Mario decided to carry out tests on them to be sure they were of equal quality—they were.

Before they departed, Mario gave the four crew members the choice to have a gold bar each or leave him to get the best possible price. They agreed in unison to leave the disposal of the bars to their boss. That way, the bars didn't have to leave France.

It was also suggested that he may require their services again in the not too distant future. If they had discovered five genuine one kilo gold bars, then it was quite certain there were more—much more!

Mario returned the *Senator Explorer* to its original mooring, then he and his crew took the tender to step ashore. Once ashore, Mario asked Eddy if he wouldn't mind taking the outboard to the chandlery deposit store and get a receipt;

he didn't want it stolen while he was in England. He and the others would meet him in the bar across the road from the Marina for a drink before going their separate ways. There were no customs formalities, as technically they had not been out of France. Before returning to England, Mario had made several attempts to discover if there were any reports in any of the local papers regarding the Brent break-in, but there had not been a word; that slightly worried him.

*   *   *

When Mario first arrived in France ahead of the crew to set things up for his 'exercise' in Switzerland, one of the many things he did was rent a deposit box at the Fleur Bank in Yvoire. His purpose for doing so was that he *may* need to deposit some of the proceeds from the Brent Depository. He would return to France after a brief visit to England, and he intended to deposit a little of the Brent proceeds at a time, leaving the rest where it was; so, he had only rented a medium-sized box. This would ultimately depend on how best it would be to dispose of the gold, as well as the artifacts. It was here he would deposit the five bars of gold from the wreck while looking for a reputable buyer, having yet again taken a photograph. In the coming days, things could change.

*   *   *

The rain was falling heavily when Mario arrived back in England, something he was not prepared for.

There was a paper stall by the taxi-rank, and Mario bought the latest edition of the *Evening Standard*. While in the back of the taxi, he checked the front page. There was no mention about the break-in at the Brent Depository, but then again, it was in Switzerland—not England—and it was five days ago.

It was late afternoon when he eventually got to his bed-sit in Elston. It was a Saturday, and his first job was to look for new accommodation. He did not like to stay in the same place for too long, ideally not too far from his favorite café, pub and restaurant, as he relied on public transport and enjoyed the comforts of eating out most of the time. This he would do on Monday. Once resettled, he would go about getting valuations for the items currently sitting at the bottom of *Lake Geneva*, first the gold bars from the Brent Depository and the ones from the wreck, then the rest of the items.

Monday mid-morning, Mario was sitting in his favorite café, having just enjoyed a late English breakfast. He was now on his second cup of coffee and browsing the property pages of the *Bedfordshire Standard*. He had put rings around four possible lettings and would make appointments to view for later in the afternoon, and if necessary, into the evening and tomorrow.

Tuesday morning, a little earlier than the day before, Mario was back at the *Greasy Spoon,* enjoying another, smaller English breakfast.

He had secured new 'digs' in the nearby village of Winston, just off the A6. References were not needed, as he had put down six months' rent up front. He was now looking at getting valuations for the gold bars, having just gotten off the phone with a Mr. Smyth of Ziptex, precious metal merchants. He would, of course, not be selling the gold bars to Ziptex; there was no point, as the bars were in France. His purpose was to secure an official valuation for when he returned to France.

*   *   *

Christina and I had just returned from spending four enjoyable days at the Queens hotel in Gibraltar, the place where we had spent our honeymoon almost two decades ago. While it was still cold in England, it was pleasantly warm in Gibraltar, and there were some excellent restaurants to be found.

My first job Tuesday morning was to check the mail and any messages on the answering machine. There was nothing too exciting in the mail, and two messages on the machine, one from Henry, welcoming me back home, and one from Max Hoffer. It seemed he had telephoned Henry, who told him I was away for a few days.

"Hello, Max," I said when I was eventually put through to his office. "You called while I was away."

"Yes, Brian, I need you to do something for me."

"I'll do my best," I replied. "What can I do?"

"I'd rather tell you in person, if you can come down to London—say tomorrow, around lunch time?"

"I'll be there, say mid-day?"

"That's good. I look forward to seeing you then," he said, at which point the phone went dead. Max was the sort of person you didn't say no to.

*   *   *

Mario was seated in the luxurious office of Mr. Smyth. On the coffee table were the two photos of the gold bars, on the back of which were a number in a circle, five and thirty-nine: five from the sunken ferry, supported to be the *Morning Mist,* and thirty-nine from the depository. There was more from the depository; these he had divided up into several bags, which he would exchange for cash a little at a time; too much at once may arouse suspicions in the market, and in more areas than one. Seated at a right angle to him was Mr. Smyth, a laptop on the coffee table facing him.

"The valuations I'm giving you are today's selling prices," Mr. Smyth pointed out.

He wrote a figure on the back of each photo. Three hundred and twenty-six thousand, two hundred and thirty-five pounds sterling for the thirty-nine bars. Forty-one thousand, eight hundred and twenty-five pounds sterling for the five bars. Not bad, Mario thought, as a bonus for the lads. He would contact them tonight with the good news.

Mario thanked Mr. Smyth and asked if he could recommend a reliable courier service, for the sake of appearances.

Back at his new digs, Mario telephoned his old crew members with the good news. He needed to keep on their better side, as he surely would have a need for them again.

He looked through his notes, where he had among other things a full list of the items extracted from the Brent depository, including: a collection of medals, medallions, coins and insignia; another collection of medals, including two dated VC medals, first class Iron Cross and the George Cross; one hundred gold Krugerands, ten each, dating 1870 to 1879; a Nero Gold Aurous coin dated around 139 AD; a small brown soft leather-velvet lined pouch containing forty cut diamonds, each a minimum of one karat; Raphael's miniature portrait of 'A Young Man'; and a commemorative Alexander III Faberge Egg studded with diamonds. He was pleased to say, the list was almost endless.

During Mario's early research into the Brent Depository, and more recently the sinking of the *Morning Mist,* he had discovered, among other things, that fifty years after the end of WWII, Swiss banks were still profiting from the Holocaust. Trains came into Auschwitz, and as the prisoners stepped off the trains, they were separated from their families, and then their possessions; gold went in one basket, jewelry in another, and clothes in another. Mario felt no guilt from his recent exercise, in fact, quite the opposite. The proceeds from the German plundering were originally to help finance the rising cost of the war.

From his own estimates, Mario had a tentative total value of forty-four million pounds sterling, plus the value of the gold. His only problem now was how to get the gold stolen from the Jews in Germany and other parts of Europe back to their rightful owners in Israel, while at the same time not raising too many suspicions.

Currently, two Israeli family members were preparing a file for a one billion Swiss franc lawsuit against the Swiss government and two banks, *Union Bank of Switzerland* and *Credit Suisse,* for refusing to return money deposited by the parents of their lost children *before* the start of WWII.

Mario had been in Switzerland checking out the Brent Depository and later emptying his box, at the same time making a final check that nothing had changed security-wise at the depository. While in Switzerland, he had gone through the procedure of enquiring the possibility of buying a bank in Switzerland. Not a regular high street bank, but one in name and address only; however, it was too expensive, and the paperwork was very time consuming. He would look at other options.

CHAPTER 15

I HAD ONLY JUST CAUGHT UP with a backload of mail, mostly bills, when it was almost time to leave the office and keep my appointment with Max Hoffer. Arriving at his bank a shade earlier than expected, I sat in the reception area. I picked up a magazine and decided to people watch, something I enjoyed doing while waiting, with little else to do.

The clock on the wall behind reception said 11:55am as I approached the desk. The middle-aged lady sitting behind the desk looked up, a pleasant smile on her face. Every time I came to visit Max Hoffer, there was a different person at the reception desk. According to the name plate on the desk this time, the lady went by the name of Louise.

"Yes, sir, what can I do for you?"

She wore a pleated grey shirt with a matching jacket over a white blouse, a multi-colored scarf around her neck, rather like a cravat. She had a pleasant smile where her mouth turned up slightly at the edges. She had high cheekbones, giving off an air of high esteem.

"Mr. Ridley to see Mr. Hoffer," I said.

"Yes," she said, looking up from what I assumed to be the senior management appointments list of the day. "Please come this way, sir."

As she stood up and walked around her desk, I could see by her long legs she was noticeably above average height. Knocking on the president's door, we entered after hearing a muffled sound. I walked over to greet Max as he came around his enormous desk, his right arm extended. I heard the door close behind me.

"Please, do have a seat."

"Thank you, Max. It's good to see you again. How are things?" I asked, leaning one elbow on the armrest.

"I'm not sure," Max replied, a frown forming on his forehead. "What about you?"

"I'm pretty good," I said, nodding my head slightly. "What do you mean about your not being sure?"

"Well, there was an article a couple of days ago in the Swiss English language newspaper, *Le Temps*. The article referred to a break-in at one of the Swiss banks."

"Oh, that doesn't sound so good," I said.

"Not when you consider the Swiss banking security is about the best in the world," Max commented. "The problem being, it wasn't just a bank in the real sense of the word, but a bank with a depository."

"A depository?" I quizzed.

"Yes, the trouble being that as such, no one knows the exact extent of what was stolen. Some boxes haven't been opened for many years, all of them rented by private individuals."

"When did this happen?" I asked.

"Over the Easter holiday, apparently," Max replied. "The trouble is, only the individual owners of the boxes know their contents. This makes it easy for the thieves to dispose of their gains, as technically none of it exists. In many cases, the owners could well be deceased. Anyway, that's not what I asked you down for today. I invited you down on a slightly delicate matter. I'm a little concerned about Herman, our vice president. Half the time, his mind isn't on his job. I'm somewhat worried that he might make mistakes. I'm also slightly concerned about his welfare."

"You mean he still isn't over the recent experience with his wife Elise, and of course himself?"

"Precisely. I had him in my office the other day to try and have a friendly chat and see if there was any way I could be of help. He didn't seem to want to open up, other than to say his wife was still suffering and hadn't played at any concert since the incident, something she would happily do—voluntarily, if necessary!"

"What is it you would like me to do, Max?"

"Henry tells me that on occasions you worked with MI5 *and* MI6. I was wondering if it was possible to see if they could help solve the issue in any way, thereby reducing the stress factor for Herman and his wife."

"Well, Max, I can ask; however, MI5 and MI6 are government agencies. As such, they can't take on any private contracts. As I said, I will, of course, ask. Maybe some discrete enquiries through the back door. I would, however, rather favor contacting Interpol. Where they're also government sponsored, they were created to combat fraud, in particular forgery and counterfeiting."

"See what you can do. If you have no luck, then I'll try Interpol, as well as the police crime division."

"I'll get on it right away," I told Max.

"Good man. Now let's go and have some lunch. I know a nice little restaurant just around the corner where they serve, among other things, the most delightful Angus steaks."

Yet again, it would seem I would need to telephone Christina to cancel dinner.

*　　*　　*

Mario had just come off the phone with one of his many contacts in France. He had been covering some ground work in preparation for his next trip to the continent, and his next move was to phone a Mr. Arlen Sayes, of CDT, gold buyers in Paris, giving them the relevant information. They had made an offer slightly better than London, subject to the gold bars being of one hundred percent, as described.

His next move was to contact a respectable auction house, but not Sotheby's or any similarly well known house. A colleague of the early days gave him a name, and the address he found easily enough in the *Yellow Pages:* Frobisher's in Mulberry Green, Harlow. Big enough and most reliable, as well as discrete

Mario gave them a call.

"With whom am I speaking?" Mario enquired.

"Mr. Benet, George Benet."

"Ah, I was given the name of a Mr. Earnest Cartwright. I was told that if I came to the auction house, I was welcome to browse through some of the house's recent catalogues."

"Mr. Cartwright is not here at the moment, but he'll be available tomorrow."

Mario made an appointment for 10:30am the following day.

Next, Mario phoned Eddy Grant. It would be a while before Mario intended to return to France, but he needed to give Eddy some advance warning: he would only need Eddy and one of the other three.

*   *   *

On my return to the office, I telephoned Henry to let him know about my meeting with Max and his request for me to seek the assistance of MI6. I also enquired about the latest on the Walter Prendigast case. There was nothing new. Tomorrow, I would be spending most of the day investigating Mr. Nigel Forester on behalf of my clients, Mr. and Mrs. Henderson. I telephoned MI6 and asked if it was possible to speak to Mr. Merryweather. I was informed he was not available.

"Could you kindly ask him to call me back when he has a moment?" I asked. "He has my number. My name is Brian Ridley."

"That won't be a problem, sir."

I caught up on a little backlog of paperwork and decided to close up in the office early, as I suspected it would be a long day tomorrow.

On my arrival home, Christina greeted me with her usual enthusiasm.

*   *   *

Mario arrived at Frobisher's auction house and was met by Mr. Benet, who told Mario Mr. Cartwright was expecting him.

"Follow me, sir," Mr. Benet said as he led Mario down a narrow corridor to an office at the far end.

Earnest Cartwright came around to the front of the desk as Mario entered the office, his right hand extended, a welcoming smile on his face. Not much more than five-feet-two inches tall, he wore heavy dark-rimmed glasses, and his matching dark hair was only visible as a couple of strips above his ears. He was wearing a grey three-piece suit and a tie that matched his hair and glass frames. Mario shook the offered hand.

"Please, take a seat," Earnest Cartwright said, indicating one of two chairs in front of his desk.

As with the gold, Mario had no intention of disposing any of the Brent collection in England. It would be much easier to have it auctioned in France, where it was currently stored; however, he needed some idea of estimated values for comparison with his and those when he got to France.

It was not his intention to auction 'all' of the Brent proceeds; the people and institutions he knew were the rightful owners would have them returned. One example was Raphael's '*Portrait of a Young Man*', circa 1909. Mario had already researched the fact that it was stolen from the Czartoryski Museum in Krakow, Poland, in or around 1945. Mario was checking out other items, but the diamonds, other jewelry and precious gems, necklaces and broaches, jade carvings, miniature mosaics and porcelain pendants, along with the coins, were all safe to go to auction. Again, the list was almost endless—Mario was pleased to say. The one thing Mario had in his possession that he was tempted to keep was none other than Hitler's passport, covering the period mid 1936–1945. How to put a value on it? There were several known 'forged' Hitler passports, mostly by the British; one in particular was stamped with a red 'J' to indicate he was a Jew for entry into British-controlled Palestine, with the number 25840 clearly stamped on it. Even an 'original' forged passport with the name 'Hitler' on it would be worth a fortune. Mario suspected the passport in his possession was genuine; otherwise, why was it stored in the Brent depository?

Mario had brought along a collection of photographs of items that would end up at auction, each with detailed information on the reverse. While Mr. Cartwright examined the photographs, checking the information against several reference books, Mario looked through some recent Frobisher catalogues.

A little over two hours later, Mario thanked Mr. Cartwright and left to return to Bedford. He was more than satisfied with the outcome of his visit to Frobisher's.

Mario was having dinner at his favorite restaurant, the Pelicano, enjoying a mixed grill when his phone rang. He usually switched it off when eating, but he had not done so on this occasion.

"Hello, Mario speaking."

"Hi, Mario, it's Eddy. When are you going back to France?"

"In about a week's time," Mario replied.

CHAPTER 16

I HAD SPENT MOST OF THE previous day investigating Mr. Forester, first on the Internet, checking his credit rating, as well as his credibility, as far as possible. It occurred to me I would need to go back to Mr. Henderson. If at all possible, I needed information, in particular where he claimed to work. Did he drive a car or use public transport? Plus any other information that might be useful.

All I had at the moment was a name, which got me his credit rating, which turned out to be not good.

I would spend most of today doing the same as yesterday. So far, I had achieved very little. I had come into the office early to complete a report for a client and was about to leave when the telephone rang.

"Mr. Ridley? Mr. Brian Ridley?"

"Speaking."

"Please hold a moment."

Seconds later, Martin Merryweather, senior operations officer from MI6, came on the line.

"Hello, Brian. How the devil are you?"

"Not so bad," I answered. "And you?"

"I'm good. I was informed that you called recently," Martin said.

"That's right, Martin. A client of mine, a Swiss Bank CEO in London, asked if MI6 might be in a position to assist him in a rather delicate situation, and likewise be helping the bank."

I went on to explain the problem, as well as how he knew about the connection between me and MI6.

"Well, as you know, Brian, MI6 isn't encouraged to get involved in matters of a private kind—unless, of course, it becomes a case of international importance."

"I appreciate what you say, Martin. I'll convey this information back to my client, and I'm sure he'll understand. I've advised an alternative—that of Interpol."

"A good idea, Brian; however, it will not hurt us to keep an eye to the ground and let you know of anything we think is relevant."

I thanked him and suggested we have lunch sometime soon—this time on me for a change!

I left the office in search of information concerning Nigel Forester.

*   *   *

Mario contacted Eddy Grant to inform him he would be heading for France in four days' time. Could he be there in a couple of days after this with Nick Burrows? This would give Mario time to re-establish the *Senator Explorer*. Eddy confirmed that he and Nick Burrows would be in France at the required time.

For the next few days, Mario was mostly at home. With the help of the Internet and catalogues, he was trying to put values on the first items that were going to auction (with the help of comments and notes from Mr. Cartwright), mostly antique jewelry, loose cut diamonds, some rather interesting micro mosaics and a large collection of bronze, silver and gold coins from countries throughout Europe—and other parts of the world. Many of them looked to be seriously ancient.

The day before his departure for France, Mario made his travel arrangements and booked his hotel, both the same as before. He later confirmed this to Eddy. Finally, he contacted the marina; after confirming who he was, he asked them to have the *Senator Explorer* made ready in the next couple of days.

Mario arrived in France, again a little before sunrise. His first stop was the car rental, open 24/7. He had bought a late evening snack, but not one for his arrival in France; so, after collecting his car, he would head for a breakfast bar. After an enjoyable breakfast—a glass of Valencia orange juice, Italian sausage with sun dried tomatoes, buttered French rolls and coffee—Mario drove to the marina, where he had left instructions for the *Senator Explorer* to be made ready and fueled. He had made a list of vitals, which would be delivered to the *Senator Explorer* while berthed at the marina.

As it was a little too early to book into the *Le Lac Leman* hotel, Mario decided to call in at 'Arlen Sayes', whose auction house and headquarters were in Paris but had offices in Messery, which was on the way to Yvoire.

After a spot of light lunch, Mario headed for the *Le Lac Leman* hotel, arriving a little before 2:00pm. He checked in and after a shower decided a nap for an hour was in order; it had already been a long day. As it turned out, his one-hour nap ended up being a little over two. At 4:30pm, he decided to repeat the activities of his last visit. A relaxing swim in the pool, possibly a short spell on the treadmill, a shower, dress for dinner, then a pre-dinner cocktail in the bar.

A board outside of the restaurant declared that there were several specialties this evening and that tomorrow was to be a special Mediterranean-themed evening.

Quite fitting, he thought. He would see what this evening had to offer.

The restaurant was becoming quite busy when Mario entered and waited at the entrance, where a red rope was suspended across a pair of upright brass stands.

The maître d'hôtel asked Mario if he was a resident or not. Mario showed the senior waiter his room key as evidence that yes, he was in fact a resident, and he would be for two or three days.

"Please come this way, sir," the waiter said.

Sitting at a table set for one (Mario concluded one place setting had been removed, as there were two chairs at the table), the waiter presented him with a brown leather bound menu that was heavier than the sizeable plate he was about to eat from.

"Do you have any recommendations?" Mario enquired. "I observed that you'd advertised some specialties at the entrance to the restaurant."

"If I may, I'd like to recommend either the 'beef medallions' in a red wine sauce, or alternatively we have roast leg of pork, with roast potatoes and apple sauce. The pork, sir, is organically farmed and free-range."

"The beef medallions sound quite exciting," Mario told the waiter, who scurried away, delighted the gentleman had selected one of his recommendations.

After dinner, Mario had another drink at the bar before retiring for the night. He rather wanted to rise early, as there were quite a lot of things to check out before his companions arrived tomorrow. Breakfast was served any time after 6:30am.

*   *   *

I had not been very successful in gaining any useful information regarding Nigel Forester. I had gone back to see Mr. Henderson, but he had not been very helpful in adding any light to his daughter's boyfriend, other than he worked in an Italian restaurant by the name of *Lui-Phips.* I decided to spend the following day in the office, most of which would be used to search the Internet yet again.

I left for home a little earlier than normal.

The following morning, I arrived at the office a little before 9 a.m. At 10 a.m., I got a call from Henry.

"Good morning, Henry," I hollered into the phone, somewhat startled by the unexpected ring. "How are we today?" I enquired.

"Well," he replied, "are you sitting down?"

"Yes, why?"

"Percival Parkinson was taken into custody last night for questioning."

"Oh, I'm not entirely surprised," I said after a long pause. "On what charges?" I asked.

"He's not being officially charged at this stage. They have seventy-two hours before they officially charge him or release him," Henry replied. "Fraud is at the top of my list, and possibly an accomplice to murder, from what the chief constable told me last night. It was the Inland Revenue who passed on the information to the Caxton police."

"Oh, so they did become involved," I said. It was more a statement than a question.

"Yes, and I believe it was with the help of your accountant friend—Bernard."

"Good for him. I'll call him later today and pass on this latest information. I'm sure he'd be delighted to know. Do you think there's any connection between Percival's arrest and the closing of the Kirby factory?" I asked.

"I don't know. A little too early to say, but I'm sure time will tell."

I reflected on the latest developments in the Parkinson case. If I was honest with myself, there would be nothing better for me than to see Mr. Percival Parkinson locked away for a very long time indeed. I always felt he was the cause of the nine months of misery I had endured after being unfairly dismissed from his brother's factory for a crime I had not committed. It would be my pleasure to visit him in prison—to point the finger at him and then laugh all the way back home. The problem was, the Parkinsons had *many* friends in very *high* places. Being accused of involvement to murder, however, was a different thing, especially if it was proved to be true.

Other than telephoning Bernard, I spent the rest of the day glued to the Internet, with some interesting results. Quite simply, Nigel Forester did not work at *Lui-Phips'*, at least not according to the restaurant's website!

*   *   *

Mario was sitting at breakfast by 7:30am; he decided on a light breakfast, as he had quite a lot to do. He would later stop for an equally light lunch. His first task was to have a plentiful supply of oxygen delivered to the *Senator Explorer* while she was still at the marina; fuel for the vessel had already been taken care of. The second task was food supplies, then he must collect the certificate, allowing him to explore the section of the lake as before. This he had applied for before leaving France the last time. After lunch, Mario would return to the hotel and make some phone calls.

He had compiled three lists: the first was the items he would send to auction; the second was the items he would *not* send to auction; and the third was the items he would return to their rightful owners, where known.

One example of returning an item to the rightful owners and not allowing it to go to auction was the miniature painting of Raphael's portrait of a young man, removed from its frame and sealed in a watertight canister. Another example was the 1909 *Alexander III Commemorative Faberge Egg,* studded with diamonds. The value of these and other similar items was of no interest to Mario, as they would be returned to their rightful owners.

In many cases, there was a generous reward for their return by their true owners from way back; however, Mario had to be careful. The original owners of the deposit boxes at the Brent Depository could discover who had removed their ill-gotten gains—if they were still alive.

Later that afternoon, Mario booked a table in the hotel's restaurant, remembering that dining this evening was a themed Mediterranean night.

He then went for a swim in the indoor pool, followed by a shower and his usual cocktail at the bar. The bar was quiet. As there was no time for a nap, he decided on a second drink.

As Mario had eaten a light breakfast, and an equally light lunch, by 6:00pm he was beginning to feel rather peckish, having had an active day. With no sign of his colleagues, Mario went in search of his reserved table.

Browsing through the evening's menu, Mario had no difficulty in making his choice: swordfish steak with potato Dauphinoise and his favorite Mediterranean grilled sun dried tomatoes. He would decide on a desert after his main meal, if he felt the need for one.

Halfway through his dinner, Mario was informed that there were two gentlemen enquiring of his presence. Good, it seemed his two colleagues had arrived.

He asked the informant if he would be kind enough to tell them he would see them in the bar shortly. He didn't feel the need for a dessert, having the pleasant taste of his dinner lingering in his mouth.

He met up with Eddy and Nick at the bar.

With a drink placed in front of him—to his surprise—compliments of his colleagues, Mario outlined the programme for the next few days.

CHAPTER 17

A STORM WAS BUILDING UP AS I returned home a little later than usual. Tomorrow, I would visit *Lui-Phips,* in an attempt to make sure the information I had just collected from the Internet was correct before reporting back to Mr. Henderson.

Over dinner, I told Christina about the Parkinson affair. She hadn't known about it until recently, as it had come under 'client confidentiality'. Now it was common knowledge.

"Bloody good show," she said, not being one to use bad language very often. "Prison is the best place for him," she added.

"I couldn't agree more," I said.

As planned, the following day I visited the *Lui-Phips* restaurant for lunch. I had been given a general description of Nigel Forester. On my arrival, I ordered a half-pint of Stella lager with a dash of lime and asked for a table. The restaurant was quiet, as it was early in the week.

"This way, sir," a short, stocky waiter said, grasping a menu and placing it under his right arm on the way.

As he pulled the chair out from the table, I thanked him and started to search the menu. The waiter then came over to take my order.

"Is my good friend Nigel Forester here, or is he on a later shift?" I asked.

"I'm sure there's no one working here by that name," the waiter replied, "however, I'll check for you."

He turned and was about to leave when I called him back.

"No need to make two trips. I'll have the spaghetti with the bolognaise sauce, please."

"Thank you, sir," the waiter said, giving me a very slight bow.

About five minutes later, the waiter returned with my lunch. Placing it in front of me, he half-whispered in my ear and said there was definitely no one working at the *Lui-Phips* by the name of Nigel Forester. It was just as I had expected.

I would report back to Mr. Henderson tomorrow, but first I would enjoy my lunch, courtesy of my client.

I implored myself to remember to phone Christina as soon as I was back in the office to let her know that a smaller dinner than normal would be good for this evening, as well as explain my reason for asking.

*   *   *

After breakfast the following morning, Mario and his two colleagues left for the marina to board the *Senator Explorer*. Once there, they would do a final check to make sure everything was on board that needed to be before departing. The vessel had already had a full check over at the marina while Mario had been in England.

Ideally, Mario would like to anchor before sunset, at the point where the *Harbor Mist* was reported to have sunk; the very same spot where he and his colleagues had found the five one kilo gold bars. His one concern was that when he eventually recovered the proceeds from the Brent Depository, it would be at risk until it arrived safely at its final destinations. The one saving grace was that they were covered by the fact that they had legal rights to search for 'sunken treasure'—where anything could be found—especially from the vessel in question.

At 4:00pm, they arrived at their destination. Dinner was very basic. A large can of vegetable soup, ample for three, with fresh French bread, followed by an ample supply of fresh fruit. As before, drinks were on the house until midnight.

The following morning after a hearty breakfast, Eddy and Nick kitted themselves out, ready to continue with the search for any gold, or other possible treasures.

Once the submersible was in the water, the two operatives could manage on their own. The boom to recover the sub on its return would remain in the outstretched position.

Once the submersible had gone below the surface, Mario was ready to proceed with the other part of his plan: using the *Senator Explorer's* launch to collect the first items on his list from the collection he had placed at the location he had marked with a pin hole on the chart.

Once at the site, Mario donned his diving gear and went in search of the heavy duty black bags.

They were not where he was certain he had dropped them—how could that be? Everything around him looked different than the last time, but of course, the gentle movement of water over time would change the terrain forever.

Mario had little choice but to return to the *Senator Explorer* and regroup his thinking. He was not a happy man; he had been very meticulous in his calculations.

Back at the mother ship, he changed out of his diving gear. Leaping up the ladder to the main deck, he headed directly for the chart table to the rear of the bridge, where he checked the chart for the area in question. Grabbing a magnifying glass from the table, he closely examined the chart.

"Well, I'll be…" Mario whispered to himself. Someone had drawn an ark using a compass, apparently to determine the course back to the marina from where he had off-loaded the gold bars from the wreck; in so doing, a second compass pin hole had been registered on the chart. This was the point Mario had gone to—the wrong one! A little over a mile-and-a-half away from his point.

There was no time to make a second attempt, but one more day would not matter. He would repeat the exercise tomorrow. In the meantime, he would start dinner while awaiting the return of the sub. Tonight's dinner would be a little more exciting than what he had last night. Mario had worked out a small menu; the idea was to buy only what was needed, again, to last no longer than a few days. Anything left over, Eddy and Nick could take home if they wanted. Tonight, Mario had planned chili-con-carne with microwave baked potato.

With the chili-con-carne already simmering and the microwave baked potatoes still a few minutes away, Mario had retreated to the ops room to go over some more valuations. He was about to check on dinner when he heard the sub return. *Good timing*, he thought, looking down at his watch.

*   *   *

The following morning after my lunch at *Lui-Phips*, I telephoned Mr. Henderson and brought him up to date on my findings concerning Nigel Forester, if that was his real name. I politely suggested that maybe he could get some additional information from his daughter. Even if anything she told her father turned out to be untrue, it would further extend the fact that Nigel Forester was not who he reported to be.

I was so busy; I had forgotten to telephone Bernard yesterday. I would do that now while enjoying my second cup of tea of the day.

*   *   *

Mario went to greet his two companions from the sub and give them a hand winching it onto the mother ship. Once the sub was settled on its cradle, Eddy and Nick heaved out a metal box from within the vessel, which was covered in a fine sand-like grit coating. Securing the metal box was an ancient lock. Eddy had little trouble removing the lock, which was well worn with age.

Opening the box revealed a hoard of coins, again some looking very old.

Mario was delighted at the discovery, but it posed a question: how to dispose of them? He did not have the time to catalogue them.

"Oh," Eddy said, "and one gold bar as well!"

Over dinner, Mario broached the subject of the coins to his two colleagues.

"I'm a little uncertain as to what to do about the coins; I don't have the time to even try to get a valuation. Most of them can't be traced back to their origin, so how do we divide them up? And who has the proceeds, us or our backer?

Nick chimed in. "Us, I should think. It would seem this is outside of your initial agreement with whoever is financing the operation, something on the side, so to speak."

"I'm inclined to agree," Eddy said.

"Except for the cost of covering our extended stay," Mario chipped in.

"We can take that away from the joint total," Eddy replied.

"How do we divide it up?" Mario asked. "There appears to be over one hundred coins in that box, each, I'm sure, with a different value!"

Nick came up with what he thought was the possible answer.

"After dinner, let's divide the coins into three lots, each taking one coin at a time, then each pick a lot. Any difference in the final value is down to chooser's luck—good or bad.

Mario had to agree that Nick's proposal was the nearest thing to being fair.

"Okay, are you happy with that, Eddy?" Mario asked.

Eddy nodded his head in agreement.

* * *

I was about to leave the office when the phone rang.

"Mr. Ridley?" the man's voice enquired.

"Speaking," I replied.

"I've been asked to let you know that Interpol has become involved in the case concerning the Goldsworth Bank."

"Who am I talking to?" I asked.

"That doesn't matter," the gentleman continued. "I've been asked to let you know of our involvement, that's all. Any information you can give us might be of considerable help."

"I'll go through the file and give you everything I've got, but who do I send it to?"

"Send it to MI6. Mark it 'GOLDSWORTH'. They, in turn, will pass it on to us!"

I replaced the receiver and sat staring at it for some time.

*   *   *

Mario informed his two friends that tomorrow was their last day in the area and that they should make the most of it. In accordance with his liking, he did not wish to stay in the same place longer than was necessary, in England, France and Switzerland—or anywhere else for that matter. He needed to get back and rescue 'some' of the items he had stored at the bottom of the lake and deliver them to their respective destinations. The time between recovery and delivery needed to be as short as possible; it would be during this period when he felt he was most vulnerable.

The following day, Eddy and Nick were out in the sub soon after daylight. After breakfast, Mario proceeded with the valuation of everything being delivered to Frobisher's auction house tomorrow.

Mid-morning, Eddy and Nick were back on the *Senator Explorer*. They had successfully recovered two more bars of gold and eleven more ancient coins, which according to Eddy and Nick were scattered on the bed of the lake. Strangely, all through their searches, there had not been a single sign of any parts of the wreck of the *Morning Mist*.

That afternoon, after an early lunch, Eddy and Nick returned to the site of the wreckage while Mario finalized his valuations. Mid-afternoon, Eddy and Nick were back, with just enough time to recharge the batteries before one final attempt, this time only salvaging a few more coins. While Eddy and Nick were out on their last trip, Mario started to prepare dinner. Tonight they would dine in style, leaving little to no food on board after tomorrow evening.

The following day at first light, Mario weighed anchor and made a course for the point *he* had made on the chart when he first dropped the gold and artifacts.

The previous day's third and last trip in the sub redeemed little other than one bar of gold. Mario told Eddy and Nick that everything gained financially on this trip would be left at the same point where he had deposited the items from the Brent Depository, to be picked up later in a different boat. He assured them both they would be back. In the meantime, he would need the assistance of Eddy and Nick to help him ashore with some of the gold and artifacts; first to Arlen Sayes with some of the gold, then on to Frobisher's auction house with some of the artifacts. Once everything had been disposed of, Mario had a final estimate, although only approximate, of sixty-six million dollars for the gold and artifacts.

CHAPTER 18

I WAS STILL STARING AT THE telephone when it rang again. I picked up the receiver.

"Brian Ridley speaking," I said into the mouthpiece.

"Hello, Brian. Max Hoffer here."

"Good morning, Max. How are you today?"

"Very well, thank you. I have some interesting news for you."

"That's a coincidence. I was just about to phone you for the same reason," I replied.

"What might that be?" he asked.

"I have just had a phone call from a gentleman who would not introduce himself. I do, however, believe he is from a department within MI6 or Interpol."

I went on to explain further, then added that I would be sending a copy of my complete file of the case on to him, including a copy of the recorded, mysterious message. I explained it had been requested.

"Very interesting," Max remarked when I finished.

"What was it you were going to tell me?" I asked.

"The bank has just received a second payment of half a million pounds sterling from our mystery man."

"Again, Max, I'm not at all surprised. I feel certain you'll get your money back—eventually, and in full. So far, he's kept his word. I don't think he would pay you a quarter of the debt unless he was going to pay you the rest."

"I'm beginning to believe you," Max commented.

"We do have a small problem, however."

"That is?" Max enquired.

"Simply that if our man is apprehended, you may not receive the balance of payments!"

"Well, Brian, as always, you have a good point. I'll give it some serious thought."

"One other thing, Max."

"That is?"

"The video images have been considerably enhanced. The authorities will be asking Herman if the other man in the video resembles the person who forced himself into his house."

"I do appreciate that. After all, I did ask you to enquire if MI6 could help us."

"Okay, Max, I'll be in touch soon."

I replaced the receiver and again stared at it, wondering who would be the next person to call.

*   *   *

Mario was more than pleased to find the gold and artifacts still in the same place where he had originally put them. Some of these items would be replaced with the latest collection from the site of the wreck, now already stored in a black heavy duty bin liner. Two lines were slung over the edge. Mario would stay on deck while Eddy and Nick recovered some of the numbered bags of gold, and likewise some of the artifacts. When Mario hoisted up the last bag of gold attached to the bottom of the lines, he lowered the bag containing the collection from the wreck.

Mario explained to Eddy and Nick the importance of getting to the marina as soon as everything was on board, thereby keeping the risk of being discovered to a minimum. The time getting to the marina from their present position was well under half an hour.

Mario had ordered a self-driven hire car to be delivered to the marina, the keys to be left at the marina's front office.

It was a little after 11:00am when the *Senator Explorer* tied up alongside berth 113 on pier number nine.

"You two bring the gold and artifacts while I get the car keys from the office. I'm told the car is a blue Ford and there aren't many cars in the car park. There never is until the weekend, and then you struggle to find a parking space."

Eddy and Nick humped the sacks of gold and artifacts to the car park while Mario raced ahead to get the keys to the car from the front office. Returning to the car park, Mario found the blue Ford, with Eddy and Nick standing by it, breathing heavily under the strain of carrying their heavy load. Mario was rather relieved when he closed the boot of the car, engulfing everything within. Eddy and Nick returned to the *Senator Explorer* to collect their personal belongings, while Mario stayed with the car.

After they had secured the vessel in readiness for hauling up onto the 'hard', they returned to the car. Mario had made a firm decision to sell the *Senator Explorer*. This type of vessel was always in demand. When he returned to the lake, he would hire a smaller boat to complete the search of the wreckage site, at the same time removing the remaining items still sitting on the bottom of the lake. Allowing for his share of the money from the wreckage site, and the sale of the *Senator Explorer,* Mario felt sure this would suffice in keeping him solvent until the next job. He suggested that his two companions accompany him to Arlen Sayes Gold Merchants to deposit the gold from their first trip. This would give them a chance to see that the price Mario had given them a while ago was genuine, other than any daily fluctuations. Once the quality of the gold had been verified, they would be paid. This would be tomorrow or no later than the day after. Later, Mario would take them to lunch before they went their separate ways.

After an enjoyable, hearty lunch—with none of them sure when their next meal would be—they split up. Eddy and Nick would be returning to England, while Mario headed for Frobisher's auction house in Paris to unload the remainder of the 'hoard'. Mario intended to stay the night in Paris, as it would be far too late by the time he returned to the *Le Lac Leman Hotel.* He found a small boutique hotel on the outskirts of Paris, the three star *Louis Blank.* He would not be dinning there, so the hotel would be fine.

After an enjoyable meal of venison with sauté potatoes, asparagus and grilled wild mushrooms at the Pablo, Mario returned to his hotel and decided on an early night, as he wanted to be up early the following morning. The following day, he would return to Yvoire to sign the papers for selling the *Senator Explorer,* and then collect his banker's draft from Arlen Sayes for the four bars of gold before checking into the *Le Lac Leman* hotel. If there was time, he would first deposit the banker's draft before checking into the hotel.

*   *   *

I had not long returned from a visit to Mr. Henderson. The additional information I was hoping for fell far short of expectations; I did, however, have the chance to tell Mr. Henderson that our Mr. Nigel Forester was not entirely as he pretended to be. I explained that I had visited the restaurant where he supposedly worked, only to find that he didn't! I suggested that maybe he should have a little in-depth conversation with his daughter and get back to me as soon as possible.

I had not heard from Henry or the police for any updates on the Parkinson affair. I had already checked the Internet and discovered that the factory in Kirby had positively closed several weeks ago. I still could not fathom why it closed after only being in operation a few years from new! There appeared to be no form of explanation on any of the websites. I decided as it was only a few miles up the road, I would go and have a look at the site, out of curiosity.

I had been sent an enhanced copy of a 'still' taken from the security video at the Goldsworth Bank. It wasn't expected that I should recognize the other man; seriously, I doubted if anyone could. The person in question was no fool. He had a dark hat pulled down low over his forehead, and he wore dark rimmed tinted glasses and a grey scarf draped around his neck and mouth, while at the same time supporting a considerable amount of 'stubble'.

An impressive cover, I thought.

*   *   *

The following morning, Mario woke up bright and early. The sun was already shining through the curtains, and it was a bright day, good for driving. He noticed the sun was moving quite high in the sky, with the fast approaching summer.

When Mario arrived for breakfast, he wasn't sure if he was one of the first or one of the last. The dining room was quiet. He took a table near a window overlooking the small garden and ordered orange juice, toast and yogurt, and finished with a black coffee.

After breakfast and paying his bill, Mario made a phone call to Frobisher's auction house to ensure everything was okay before heading back to Yvoire. He was assured it was and that his collection would be entered in the catalogue this very day for the next rare antiques and collector's auction in ten days' time. He had decided *not* to return the *Alexander III Commemorative Egg*. He had discovered that the Russians had been doing exactly what the Germans had been doing near the end of WWII—looting; in this instance, artifacts from Europe to Russia. It had been reported that statues and paintings were being taken to the border by truck before being transferred to trains heading for Russia. He was unable to get solid information in this area, so he would therefore hold on to the 'Egg' until he could be certain.

CHAPTER 19

I T WAS EARLY AFTERNOON WHEN Mario arrived back in Yvoire. Before going to the marina, he would call into Arlen Sayes gold merchants to see if his banker's draft was ready; it was. There would be more, as they sold the Brent gold a little at a time.

After some formal paperwork, he decided to deposit the draft in his bank before proceeding to the marina.

Mario felt much happier once the money was in his account: a little over twenty-one million, plus additional funds of forty-one thousand GBP (the first five bars from the wreck), to be shared; another bridge crossed in his steadily developing operation. He would dispose of the more recent four gold bars from the wreck later, after informing Eddy and Nick.

Now mid-afternoon, Mario sat in the marina sales office to discuss the sale of the *Senator Explorer.*

"As you know," Mario told the sales manager, "I purchased the vessel from you not so long ago for 1.7 million euros; therefore, I'm willing to accept any offers over 1.6 million euros."

"That seems quite reasonable," the manager offered. "If you'll sign these papers and leave me your address or contact number, I'll get back to you."

Mario was reluctant to leave his address. He left his international mobile phone number, along with the proof of ownership papers. This he had done when he received the owner transfer papers and delivery of the vessel. The manager seemed quite happy with this; after all, as Mario had rightly pointed out—they had sold the vessel to him not that long ago, and he had maintained it in excellent condition, the most recent tune up being a little over a week ago.

* * *

I had spent most of the morning surfing the Internet to see if I had missed any gainful information regarding Mr. Nigel Forester. I had managed to find out that his credit rating was far from good and his address was unknown. I was considering other options when the phone rang.

"Brian, me boy," Henry's voice hollered in his usual jovial way. "How are you today?"

"I'm good," I said. "And you?"

"Not complaining," he replied in an uncertain tone. "I thought you might like to know Percival Parkinson has been 'officially' arrested and charged with embezzlement. The police are still uncertain regarding Parkinson's accountant—insufficient evidence—but they'll continue their investigations."

"Oh," I replied. "It would seem, then, that *is* the reason for the factory in Kirby closing. I always found it very unusual that a brand new purpose built factory would close in such a short time after opening. What do you think, Henry?"

"I agree," he replied, "very suspicious indeed. The police know you once worked for the Parkinson outfit, and of course were originally called in by Walter Prendigast to investigate suspicious accounting discrepancies within the company. They may well be in touch with you for any information you may be able to give them."

"Thank you, Henry. I'll be here." I also told Henry I had decided to take a drive over to Kirby and have a look at the Parkinson factory.

*   *   *

By the time Mario had finished at the marina, it was late afternoon; so, he made the decision to stay at the *Le Lac Leman* hotel an extra night. The last few days had been quite exhaustive, and he felt like he could do with a brief rest. First, though, he desperately needed to freshen up.

The sun was falling rapidly onto the horizon when Mario arrived at the hotel. It was still only very early summer. Weather-wise, it had been very pleasant, and now Mario was ready to relax. On the way up to his room, he had a glance at the 'specials of the day' at the entrance to the restaurant; they advertised a themed Mexican evening.

Interesting, he thought.

Mario had decided to check through his one-third share of the coins from the wreck, his total share coming to thirty-four coins. There were quite a few early dated gold and silver coins that had the appearance of being of considerable value. He had brought his catalogues from the *Senator Explorer,* not wishing to leave them on board, as the vessel was now up for sale. He would use the next couple of days to check them out. After some thought, Mario considered that the collection of coins—one hundred in total—must have been put together for a good reason, and therefore of considerable value!

After an enjoyable dinner, as always at the *Le Lac Leman,* of Mexican Salad with tortilla croutons, followed by Mexican Beef Chili and Potatoes, Mario retired to the bar to cool down his mouth and throat.

After a couple of cooling 'Rum and Cokes', he returned to his room, where he spent an hour checking the coins from the wreck before retiring for the night, determined not to get up early.

The following morning, he arose to sunlight, again shining from a clear sky. The time was 9:00am, and the restaurant closed for breakfast at 10:30am, giving him plenty of time with no need to hurry. After breakfast, he returned to his room, picked up his laptop, collected his catalogues on coins, and went down to the reception, which was spacious and comfortable, and he could connect to the Internet there, should he need to. He continued cataloguing the coins as much as possible. From the time spent the previous evening, the collection was exceeding his expectations; some he had not managed to value. At a little after 1:00pm, he had gone as far as he could go.

Mario was not interested in lunch, allowing him to have a good appetite for dinner. He made two decisions: one was that he would need to get professional valuations of the eighteen coins he could not find values for; secondly, he would contact Eddy and Nick to suggest they let him do the same for them. When he next saw them, he would explain why he had decided to investigate the values before parting with them. They agreed.

One very interesting coin Mario discovered was not gold or silver, but copper-nickel. It was a 1933 British penny. Mario remembered from his earlier days when he was a keen stamp and coin collector that the 1933 penny was classed as 'extremely rare'. He discovered while researching the coin on the Internet that only between 7 and 10 were actually minted; the certainty of actually how many was never recorded. The locations of six were known. One was in the *Royal Collection,* one in the *Royal Mint Museum.* Another was under the foundation stone of an undisclosed building of the same year. Three were in private collections. The whereabouts of the remaining possible four were unknown. The value, depending on their condition, was upwards of forty-five thousand pounds sterling. Mario decided his was a very good sample. What, therefore, was the value of the other ninety-nine coins?

Delighted with the results of his morning's work, Mario stopped off at the bar for a lunch time drink before returning to his room. After a short nap, he decided to spend some time working out before a leisurely swim, after which he considered that a second drink at the bar was in order. Back in his room, Mario phoned Frobisher's in Paris and made an appointment for the following day. While doing his workout, he had decided that to call in on them on the way back to England would be a good idea. He would leave all the coins with them while the additional fifteen unidentified items were being valued. He would also leave the Alexander III commemorative egg with them. He did not want to cross any borders with it.

* * *

I had just returned from seeing a new client and was going through their file when the phone rang.

"Mr. Ridley?" the voice asked.

"Speaking," I replied.

"This is Inspector Hatfield, from Caxton CID. We need to ask you a few questions regarding a Mr. Percival Parkinson, if that's all right. We've been led to believe by one of their solicitors that you were employed by their late accountant *and* that at one time you worked for Parkinson's younger brother in his Kirby factory."

"That's correct," I replied, "with the exception that I left the company before it moved to Kirby."

"Is it possible, Mr Ridley that you could come to the police station? We feel you might be able to assist us with our enquiries."

* * *

Mario ate in the hotel restaurant that evening. There was no themed evening, but that did not matter; the hotel had a fine a la carte menu. Mario ate quite late, enjoying a meal of mini beef wellingtons with sauté potatoes and baby carrots. After dinner, he retired to the lounge bar, ordered a Brandy Alexander, and read through the *Tribune* English language newspaper. He retired early; tomorrow would be a long day, and he would request an early morning call at the reception.

The following morning at 7:30am, Mario got his wake-up call.

After a light breakfast, he paid his bill and departed for Frobisher's in Paris.

Mario left the coins with the auctioneer with instructions to calculate a value so reserves could be put in place, along with the commemorative egg. He did not tell them he had valued some of the coins; this way, he would be able to see how accurate he had been.

It was mid-afternoon when Mario had completed his business at Frobisher's. He stayed in France overnight and traveled on to Liechtenstein the following morning, first returning his hired car. He had given much thought about whether or not to buy a bank in France, Switzerland or Liechtenstein. France was very difficult, Switzerland very expensive. Liechtenstein, a small country on the border of Switzerland, was welcoming with open arms. The bank in question was not a commercial bank, but a bank in name only, nonetheless quite above board. The Hasher Bank PLC—with an address to go with it—it did not cost too much. With such large quantities of money involved, he did not want to run the risk of investigative authorities prying into the possibilities of money laundering. Banks in Liechtenstein were known to be very discrete. In addition, the final recipient bank needed to think the incoming funds were at least 'part payment' for gold and valuables stolen from the Jews during WWII. This was currently being negotiated between the Senate Banking Committee, the many Swiss banks involved, and the World Jewish Congress. So far, almost $500 million had been paid out by the various Swiss banks; this fell way below the estimated $3.5 billion *still* owing.

CHAPTER 20

MARIO BOOKED AN EARLY FLIGHT to St. Gallen-Alternrhein Airport in Switzerland. From the airport, he got a taxi to the agent's office in Liechtenstein. From there, he could pick up the keys for the Hasher Bank. He had booked an appointment for late in the morning. The agent told Mario that there would be someone in the office when he arrived. He gave the driver the address, then sat back and tried to relax for the little under one-hour journey. Liechtenstein was one of only six countries in the world that did not have an airport within its boundaries.

Sure enough, when Mario arrived at the agent's office, there was someone available so he could complete the outstanding paperwork.

Once satisfied everything was in order, Mario returned to the St. Gallen-Alternrhein Airport, from where he would book himself on the next available flight back to London.

By the time Mario arrived in London, it was late afternoon. Unlike the last time he got back from France when it had been raining, the sky was blue, and although the sun was shining, the air was still cool.

*   *   *

"Mr. Ridley, thank you for coming in to see us. Hopefully, we won't keep you long."

I was at the police headquarters in Caxton for almost two hours. I eventually returned to my office, satisfied that I had done my part in assisting the police as best I could. I got the impression from the police that Percy Parkinson was not guilty of murder, but he was believed to be involved somewhere.

Back in the office, I gave Henry a call.

"Hello, Henry. I just thought I'd let you know I've just spent almost two hours at Caxton police HQ. No problems. They were grateful for my assistance."

"Good for you, me boy," Henry replied. "I have nothing to report from this end. Keep in touch."

I promised I would.

*   *   *

The following morning, after Mario's return to England, he sat in his favorite café having breakfast and telephoned Eddy with the information about the coins. It was another warm and sunny early summer's day. The warmth was feeling most comfortable, shining on his face through the café's glass window.

Eddy was surprised at the news, but very pleased. Mario explained why he had changed his mind about getting valuations. With some spare time on his hands while waiting to complete his business, he had glanced through the thirty-four coins in his possession. He recognized some of the coins and thought it best to check the value before disposing of them. He added that he was waiting for a total valuation on his share. Also, he had put up his two colleagues' coins but was, as always, careful not to give too much away.

After telephoning Eddy, Mario transferred the money to both Eddy and Nick's bank account, for their share of the gold discovered from the wreck: ten thousand eight hundred GBP each.

Mario decided—all things considered—that he would return to France for the auction.

The week following the fine arts auction, there was a Rare Stamp and Coin auction. He would travel to France two or three days before the Fine Arts auction, giving him time to enter the coins in the Rare Stamp and Coin auction whilst being present at the Fine Arts auction at the same time.

In the meantime, he would start looking for somewhere else to live. It would be about time to move on when he returned from his next trip to France. Also, it would soon be time to make the third half million payment to the Goldsworth Bank.

The next couple of days, Mario spent time drafting up a letter to accompany the first of several payments he would be sending to the National Bank of Israel, one of the banks authorized by the 'World Jewish Congress' to receive payments on behalf of the beneficiaries. They had a special account for receiving and distributing funds to qualified recipients.

*   *   *

I was due to visit Max Hoffer to give my now monthly report. First, I telephoned the bank to confirm.

"May I speak to Max Hoffer?" I asked the receptionist when she picked up the phone.

"Who's calling, please?"

I gave her my name.

"One moment, please."

A few moments later, Max came on the line.

"Good morning, Brian. How are you today?"

"I'm fine," I said. "And you?"

"Pretty good, thank you."

"I'm phoning to confirm my meeting with you, and to give you my monthly report," I told him, "although there's very little to report," I hastily added.

"Come down anyway, we can have a spot of lunch together afterwards."

"Is late morning tomorrow okay?" I asked.

"That'll be fine," he said, and then the line went dead.

I decided Max enjoyed the opportunity of having lunch with me, a welcome break to get away from financial conversations he must be used to all day.

The following morning, sitting across the desk from Max, I tendered my report.

"There's not much to say," I told him. "Very few leads and the ones I had have all come to a dead end—dried up, so to speak!"

"Well, I invited Herman to bring his wife, Elise, into the office," Max said. "I thought a little friendly chat between the three of us would do no harm. Elise has almost fully recovered from what she calls her traumatic ordeal. Also, she's now back playing the piano at concerts. I explained we had a private investigator on the case, as well as the police working in the background, and Interpol was also now involved. Then I mentioned the remark you made last time we spoke. If this person is found and arrested, the bank will not get the rest of the money back. Needless to say, Herman was quick to grasp the situation."

"Well, the way things are going," I interjected, "it looks like this person, whoever he is, won't be found. He's been most meticulous in his planning."

"Quite so. That's what I'm beginning to think also."

It was agreed that we drop the investigation. I had not heard from the person who had sent me a copy of the enhanced videotape of Herman and the 'mystery' man entering the bank, certain though he had been that he recognized the person with Herman the night of the forced entry. Max agreed he would not—possibly could not—cancel the investigation, but he would not press the issue further. I told him I would send a final bill, after which we went to lunch.

* * *

Mario had read and re-read the two-page letter he had drafted up to send to the World Jewish Congress. On receipt of the letter, it was most important that the organization felt the money contained within *was* from various organizations dedicated to returning money rightfully owed to the Jewish community from whom it was stolen in the first place, both before and during WWII. He had used his own bank's letterhead, for appearances sake. Accompanying the letter would be a banker's draft made payable to the World Jewish Congress. The final amount as yet was far from certain, as the gold and artifacts were being dealt with a little at a time.

The following day, Mario made preparations to return to France. This time he would fly, as he would be staying in Paris. First he would locate a respectable hotel with a five-star restaurant, and then he would inform Frobisher's where he was staying.

CHAPTER 21

MARIO HAD PRE-BOOKED AND PAID for his hotel in Paris before leaving England, the *Le Royal Monceau-Raffles,* situated on the Champs Elysees in the centre of Paris, and not very far from Frobisher's auction house. He had been assured that the two restaurants in the hotel were of the highest standard; at three hundred and nineteen GB pounds a night, *excluding* breakfast, he expected it should be. When Mario was out of England, he considered that fine food and good wine were of the utmost importance, especially in his line of work. All things considered, he thought it a small indulgence; after all, his next hotel could be a no-star prison cell!

Mario arrived at the Charles de Gaulle Airport at 3:10 Wednesday afternoon. He'd had breakfast before leaving England and wasn't interested in any lunch, again building up an appetite for an early evening dinner. He hailed a taxi and gave the driver instructions as to which hotel he was staying at.

The hotel was exactly as described on the Internet: stately and elegant from the outside, and most luxurious on the inside! Apart from the extra large indoor swimming pool, the hotel boasted 149 luxury rooms, a cinema, ballroom, a wine bar and a night club, as well as the reception lounge and bar.

The hotel took up a corner position at an intersection on the Champs Elysees. A typical Parisian building of the early 1900s, it was most magnificent in its exterior detail, and typical of Parisian architecture. The interior was of superior elegance. As with the outside, the interior had many carvings, again resembling the early 1900s. The drapes at the floor to ceiling windows were of a very fine fabric and superior quality. Mario suspected they were woven especially for the hotel. Between the windows were oil paintings of well known Parisian scenes.

At the check-in desk, Mario was handed a fax from Frobisher's, suggesting he give them a call. He went directly to his room, called Frobisher's, and spoke to a Mr. Graveshaw.

"Good afternoon, Mr. Petri. Welcome back to France. I have some interesting information for you that I didn't wish to put in the fax we sent to your hotel."

"Thank you kindly," Mario replied.

"The estimated value of the thirty-four coins you left with us is five hundred and forty-four thousand pounds; however, in these circumstances we expect to realize a higher figure at auction. Some people get into a bit of a fight to be the winner if there is more than one person bidding after the same item, particularly if it's rare."

Mario sat down.

"I'll call in tomorrow, early morning. We can discuss entering them into your forthcoming rare coin and stamp auction next week, yes?"

"Yes, of course. "We look forward to seeing you tomorrow, then."

Mario unpacked his case, took a shower, and then lay down for a nap. What now concerned him was the value of the coins Eddy and Nick had. They had been evenly distributed, having thirty-three coins each against Mario's thirty-four. If theirs were of a similar value, even allowing for Mario to have the luck of getting the highest valued coin in the collection, it still allowed for Eddy and Nick to be in receipt of several hundred thousand pounds. This could present problems for Mario. With the police keeping a watchful eye on Eddy—and who knows who else—they would be extremely suspicious if Eddy started splashing unusually large amounts of money about.

Giving the problem considerable thought, Mario came up with an idea.

Neither Eddy nor Nick knew the value of Mario's share of the coin collection any more than they did their own; he had only just found out himself. He would suggest that he had their coins valued by the same firm. When Mario had the total value of the one hundred coins, he would take the thirty-four highest valued coins for himself; the remaining sixty-six, he would divide equally into two. He would keep the lower valued coins separate from the higher valued coins. This way, he would have a genuine sales receipt from the auctioneers to give Eddy and Nick. This would mean delaying the auction of his coins, but that would not matter.

Looking at the bedside clock, he decided that at 7:10pm it was time to dress for dinner.

After having his usual pre-dinner drink in the Paris City Walk bar, Mario went directly to the Congress dining room. A senior waiter at the entrance to the dining room asked for his room number. After showing the waiter his key fob, Mario was shown to a table centrally placed within the dining room.

He took his time browsing the menu. The prices signified a very high standard—he hoped so.

After careful deliberation, Mario selected the filet beef mignon in a red wine sauce, medium to well done, with asparagus and baby Jersey Royal potatoes. While waiting, he asked for the wine waiter. After checking the wine list, he selected a bottle of Cabernet Sauvignon to accompany his dinner. He would have half this evening and finish the other half tomorrow.

It was a good fifteen minutes before his meal arrived, something Mario always saw as a good sign.

The beef mignon was tender and succulent; the vegetables were done to perfection, the wine delightful. He had been on a serious diet while in England, in preparation for this trip.

He signed the tab with delight.

Having a Brandy and Benedictine at the bar before retiring for the night, Mario returned to his room a very satisfied person.

*   *   *

I was sitting in a two-seater settee in the middle of Mr. Henderson's office, enjoying a cup of surprisingly good English tea, by office tea standards. Mr. Henderson was sitting opposite me, seemingly equally enjoying a cup of cappuccino coffee, both delivered by his seemingly efficient secretary.

I had just finished briefing him on the case concerning his daughter's boyfriend; I used the term 'boyfriend' rather than 'fiancé', as I suspected they were not engaged.

I had managed to find out a little more about him than had been possible earlier, with a little added help from Mr. Henderson himself. I had already told him he did not work at the *Lui Phips* restaurant—and never had, according to the restaurant staff. I had also told him his credit rating was worse than poor. I had found out his address from the credit rating people, but on further investigation, he no longer occupied the dwelling! There was no forwarding address. I had tried to find out which bank he used, if any, with the help of the credit rating company. No such luck in that area either, a case of confidentiality. I had tried to spend a day, or at least part of a day, following him, something I was not an expert at. But then, Nigel Forester was not expecting to be followed; however, where to start? I had to find him before I could follow him! I had suggested to Mr. Henderson that he inform his daughter he was not what he pretended to be. If necessary, he could confront Nigel Forester in person.

Mr. Henderson thanked me and told me he would take it from here on. I told him if there was anything further he thought I could do, not to hesitate to ask. I then left for home.

The following day, I had a lunch appointment with Martin Merryweather, at my invitation. My excuse had been to let him know we were no longer pursuing the Goldsworth Bank robbery case—If that's what you could call it—and I explained the reason why. I thanked Martin for MI6's modest endeavors in assisting with the problem. As he had pointed out, MI6 could not be seen getting involved in private cases of any nature. In fact, it was rather the opposite;

there had been occasions when *they* had gotten in touch with me.

Tomorrow was Friday. Before leaving the office for home and the weekend, I would call Henry and bring him up to date with the latest happenings, not that there were many. With only two clients at the present time, a situation with which I was more than happy, I could afford to enjoy the 'whole' weekend off. Things had been hectic until now, and I knew Christina would be happy.

Then the phone rang!

CHAPTER 22

MARIO WAS UP BRIGHT AND early, after the previous evening's most delightful meal. He had a very light breakfast in the city before proceeding on to Frobisher's. Mr. Graveshaw greeted him, while at the same time apologizing for the limited amount of time he could offer Mr. Petri. He went on to explain that the auction would be starting at 10:30am, and he of course would need to be present.

"However, there is time for a coffee, if you would care to join me?"

"I do understand, and thank you, yes," Mario told Mr. Graveshaw.

"I'll be brief. The coins you've valued for me, I have sixty-six other coins for which I need valuations also."

Mario then remembered the more recent coins from the wreck.

"That sixty-six may be nearer eighty. I'll need to check. I therefore need to delay entering the existing coins into next week's auction, but hopefully I'll be ready for the following one."

At that moment their coffee arrived, while at the same time Mr. Graveshaw was presented with a slim folder. He handed the folder over to Mario, along with the coffee. Mario opened the folder and saw that the folder contained a list of the thirty-four coins recently valued by them. He was most surprised to note that the 1933 penny was *not* the most valuable coin in the collection; rather, a 1642 Charles I British gold coin was estimated at near 66.000 pounds sterling.

Mr. Graveshaw informed Mario that the following Rare Coin and Stamp auction would be in four weeks, after the coming one next week.

"Five weeks from now, I'll be ready," Mario assured Mr. Graveshaw.

Mario could not remember exactly how many coins or gold bars were discovered on the last visit to the site of the wreck, but he could soon check. This would mean returning to the site where he had 'dropped off' the remaining last find.

"Thank you, Mr. Graveshaw," Mario said. Finishing his coffee, he stood up and shook his host's hand. "You've been most helpful."

Mario left the auction house deep in thought. He was further concerned about the rising value of the coin collection from the wreck of the *Harbor Mist.*

Tomorrow, he would check out of the *Royal Monceau Raffles Hotel*, hire a car, and return to the *Le Lac Lemon* in Yvoire.

Back in his Paris hotel, Mario had plenty of time to take a nap, followed by thirty minutes on the treadmill in the exercise hall, and then a long shower back in his room. Again, he had not bothered to have any lunch, relishing the thought of another enjoyable dinner.

On his way to the cocktail bar, he ordered a hire car from 'Hertz' for early the following day.

The cocktail bar was quiet when Mario entered, with only one other couple present. He picked up a complimentary newspaper while passing the reception, ordered a Piña Colada at the bar, and took his drink and paper to a nearby table; he was in no hurry. He continued to ponder the minor problem of the increasing value of the coin collection and what this would present.

Mario enjoyed the other half bottle of cabernet sauvignon from the previous evening with his dinner, prime organic roast leg of Welsh lamb accompanied by baby roast potatoes, Brussel sprouts and asparagus.

After his usual after-dinner brandy in the bar, Mario retired for the night after booking another early morning call.

The following morning, up bright and early, Mario decided again to forgo breakfast; instead, he would stop halfway to Yvoire for 'brunch'. Paying his bill, a little under the equivalent of one thousand GB pounds, he left the hotel, still deep in thought.

*   *   *

As usual, I was about to leave the office for home when the phone rang. I picked up on the fourth ring.

"Hello, Brian speaking."

"Hello, Brian. It's Henry. Sorry to phone so late in the day, but I thought you may like to know a preliminary hearing date for Mr. Parkinson Sr. has been set for next Wednesday, should you like to be present."

"Thank you, Henry. I most certainly would."

When I arrived home, I told Christina the latest news. She smiled up at me, and when I told her I would be going along, she asked if she could come, too.

"Certainly," I said. All things considered, I wouldn't have it any other way."

*   *   *

It was mid-afternoon when Mario arrived in Yvoire. He drove directly to the hotel *Le Lac Lemon.*

"Good to have you with us again, Mr. Petri," the concierge said to Mario as he entered.

After checking in for two nights, Mario went directly to his room and decided on a much needed rest before dinner. First, however, he needed to telephone the marina and hire a diving boat for a few hours early the following morning.

Apart from having a diving certificate, he also had a license to skipper any vessel up to one hundred feet in length.

It was 7:30pm on the dot when Mario entered his favorite dining room. This was the part of the day he enjoyed. Taking his time perusing the menu, Mario invited the waiter to offer any recommendations he might have.

"Yes sir. I do recommend the roast leg of pork with mustard and honey glaze and fresh stir-fried mixed vegetables, or…"

"No, the roast leg of pork sounds fine," Mario replied, closing the menu. Before the waiter could continue, he handed the menu to him, a happy smile on his face.

After a dinner he again thoroughly enjoyed, Mario had a cognac in the bar before retiring early. He needed an early night, as it was to be an early start tomorrow; not a long day, but a hard day.

Mario put in for an early morning call on the way up to his room.

*   *   *

Wednesday morning, I did not go to the office; instead, Christina and I went directly to the Crown Court in Caxton. I had telephoned Henry, in case he would like a lift. He kindly pointed out that his office was purposely only a stone's throw away from the courthouse and the walk would do him good.

This morning's hearing was for Percival Parkinson to plead guilty or not guilty, for bail to be refused or granted, and thus to decide on a date for the actual hearing. It was rumored Mr. Parkinson would plead not guilty.

The courthouse was already full to near bursting when Christina and I arrived. Percival was a very prominent person in Caxton, the multi-millionaire owner of a group of factories whose headquarters were in Caxton, employing several hundred local people. We managed to get two seats at the rear. Having been seated only a couple of minutes, I caught sight of Henry standing up and facing the back of the court, waving a rolled up newspaper in his hand. He beckoned for us to come forward, as he had kindly reserved a couple of seats for us—a lawyer's privilege, I assumed.

"Lovely to meet you again, Mrs. Ridley, this time under more pleasant circumstances."

It was not long before the courtroom was called to order and the noise of chatter gradually fell to silence as the presiding judge entered.

"Please rise for the Honorable Judge William. B. Henderson."

Once His Honor was seated, proceedings began.

*   *   *

It was barely daylight when Mario got his early morning call. Feeling fresh after what he felt had been a good night's sleep, he went into the bathroom. After a brief shower, he dressed.

Driving to the marina, Mario presented his credentials, including his diving certificate; it was a necessity to produce your diving certificate if you hired diving equipment, the certificate number being recorded on their copy of the invoice. He collected the diving boat, complete with equipment. Mario was making good time. It would take him less than an hour to arrive at his designated place and collect the two small bags of gold and coins from the bottom of the lake, left from their second visit to the site of the wreck. Three-and-a-half hours later, he was back at the marina. Relieving himself of the diving boat and equipment, he collected his car and headed directly to Arlen Sayes area office to dispose of the last of the gold.

It was mid-afternoon when Mario returned to the hotel. He felt like a rest, but he decided to resist; instead, he would have another 'very' early night, as he had the long drive back to Paris tomorrow.

After taking his usual pre-dinner cocktail in the bar, Mario headed for the restaurant and was escorted to a table. When he was presented with the menu, he was pleased to see the waiter was the same as the previous evening.

"Good evening," the waiter politely said, recognizing Mario. "What shall it be this evening, sir?"

Mario looked up at the waiter. "Last evening, I didn't give you the chance to name the alternative to the 'glazed pork'," he said. "Perhaps you would be kind enough to tell me now—and if it's available this evening?"

"Certainly, sir. The alternative was filet of beef with Roquefort cheese, and yes, sir, it's still on the menu."

"Now that sounds rather delightful. I'll be more than happy to give it a try."

Needless to say, again Mario was not disappointed.

Returning to the bar for his post-dinner cognac, he returned, as he promised himself he would, to his room for an early night, after first putting in for another early morning call. Before turning in, Mario listed the one hundred and fifteen coins, less the thirty-four already valued, he would present to Mr. Worthington tomorrow.

The following morning, Mario was up at the morning call and decided he would have a light breakfast before making his departure, thereby foregoing lunch.

Having packed most of his clothes last night before retiring, he placed the rest of his clothes and toiletries in his hold-all and left for the reception.

Once behind the wheel of his hired car, he left Yvoire and headed back towards Geneva, bypassing the city and turning onto the E15, headed northwest to Paris. It was a little after 2:00pm when Mario arrived at Frobisher's, where he presented Mr. Worthington with the coins.

"I would be most grateful if you could value these eighty-one coins, as before," Mario requested. He did not feel confident enough to value the coins himself, as he was not an 'expert' in that area, just a one-time collector. Anyway, he didn't have the time, and his coin catalogues were now in England.

"I'll get our coin expert onto it straightaway," Mr. Worthington announced. "It'll probably take the best part of a couple of days."

"That'll be fine," Mario replied and handed Mr. Worthington a phone number where he could be reached.

Mario intended to stay at the same boutique hotel where he had stayed during his first visit to Paris; however, he had been so impressed with his last visit to the *Le Royal Monceau Raffles* that he made a last-minute decision to return there instead.

*　　*　　*

As expected, Percival Parkinson pleaded not guilty. It was now down to the court to set a date for the preliminary hearing. First, however, there was the question of bail.

"Your Honor, my client has requested that he be allowed bail," the defense lawyer announced, "on the grounds that he has a rather large processing factory to run and is therefore unlikely to jump bail."

The prosecution, however, had different ideas on the subject.

"Your Honor, Mr. Parkinson is a multi-millionaire and could therefore walk away from his factory *and* home and not look back."

"Point taken," His Honor returned. "Bail is refused."

A date was set for 'preliminaries' in eight weeks' time. By this time, a jury would be established.

Mr. Parkinson left the courtroom grim-faced. The idea of confinement for a minimum of a further eight weeks did not amuse him; however, it certainly did me!

I was not sure whether Percival saw me in the courtroom. He certainly would not recognize my wife or Henry, having never met them. I rather hoped, though, he had seen me; if he had, he would have noticed the rather large grin on my face.

We were well into the summer. By my calculations, Max would soon be receiving the third payment on the unofficial loan.

*   *   *

Mr. Worthington was true to his word. Exactly two days after Mario had left the coins at Frobisher's; he received a call from them suggesting he come over to the auction house, as the valuation was complete.

With the original 34 coins already valued, 1.7 million pounds sterling was the total value, Mario was informed when he was sat comfortably across from Mr. Worthington.

Mario could not believe what he had just heard. Delightful news that it was, it was going to give him one enormous headache!

"Can I see the list?" Mario asked.

"Certainly," Mr. Worthington said, handing over a clear plastic folder with two A4 sheets of printed paper inside. "You can keep that copy for your records. I would remind you that the figure of 1.7 million pounds could be considerably higher," he added.

Mario briefly glanced down the list. As far as he could see, the least expensive coin was estimated at two thousand three hundred pounds. He thanked Mr. Worthington, telling him he would be back tomorrow with a list of how many of the coins were to be entered in the upcoming auction.

His next visit was to a shop specializing in the *sale* of coins.

There were thirty coins in the existing collection he could afford to enter into the auction on behalf of Eddy Grant and Nick Burrows. He would need to find thirty-six extra coins to show the correct number for Eddy and Nick—at an 'acceptable' auction price. Mario could not afford to let Eddy and Nick have one third of 1.7 million pounds, or anywhere near it. There would be too many prying eyes ready to pounce as soon as they started spending the money—and spend it they would!

Then there were the fifteen extra coins found during the last visit to the site of the wreck. Mario visited three dealers before he had purchased the required amount of coins of a considerably lower value—but still very collectable.

Returning to his hotel, Mario decided on a little exercise before dinner; not too much, as it had been quite an exhaustive day. After dinner, he would return to his room and draw up three lists of coins: one for Eddy, one for Nick, and a third for the other fifteen coins, the money from all these to be evenly divided between the three of them—less Mario's expenses, of course.

CHAPTER 23

I T HAD TAKEN MARIO ALMOST four hours to compile the three lists. When he had finished, he was confident he had got it right—well, as near as was humanly possible.

The following day, Mario returned to Frobisher's with the list of coins. Among them were the thirty-three new ones. Included in Mario's list were thirty-three of the lowest valued coins of the original collection.

Handing the coins over to Mr. Worthington, he pointed out that in the list there were thirty-three additional coins that didn't need valuing, as he already knew the values, and thirty-three of the existing coins being held by the auction house. They were to be entered as three separate lots: Eddy, Nick, and the fifteen coins found during the last expedition. The remainder would be held by Frobisher's while Mario decided whether to enter them individually or as a collection.

Mario returned to his hotel a mentally exhausted man, hoping for a very relaxing evening.

On his arrival back at the hotel, he learned the marina had called. A message at the reception desk said he was to contact them. Being a marina, their offices were open until quite late. Mario called them from the hotel.

"Mr. Petri, one moment please," a voice said at the other end. A moment later, the sales manager came on the line.

"Mr Petri, we're pleased to inform you we've made a successful sale of the *Senator Explorer* on your behalf, and I hasten to add, at your asking price. You were lucky enough to have more than one interested person, which helped keep the price up."

"Thank you for your endeavors," Mario said. "Do you need me to come to the marina?"

"That won't be necessary," the manager replied.

*   *   *

The following day, Mario drove to the airport, returned his hired car, and flew to London. He would return to Paris in a few days' time in readiness for the auction of the coins and collect the few last remaining items still at the bottom of the lake.

While in England, Mario brought Eddy and Nick up to date on his progress regarding the sale of the coins and gold from the wreck. He also told them he would be returning to France for the sale of the coins, and then bringing back the proceeds from the sale on his return to England.

Both Eddy and Nick thanked Mario for the deposit of funds into their accounts from the sale of the gold bars from the first visit to the wreck.

It was three days later when Mario arrived back in France; he had stayed in England just long enough to tie up a few loose ends. The auction had gone well. Both Eddy and Nick had realized well over a five figure sum, plus one-third of the other fifteen coins—still to come. They were more than happy with their share. In both cases, it was by far much lower than one-third of 1.7 million.

While he remembered, Mario made the third payment to the Goldsworth Bank—it was now August.

While Mario had been sorting out the coin auction, he had also been sorting out the remaining artifacts—a little at a time. He had been careful about what went through the auction and what didn't. He had even put a bet on with himself as to which item would fetch the highest price!

*   *   *

It had been almost two months to the day when Christina and I found ourselves back at the Caxton Crown Court. As before, we were sitting alongside Henry. The hearing had proceeded for ten days before the prosecution called for a temporary adjournment. During the questioning, the defense for Mr. Percival had disclosed certain information to the court, but not to the prosecution; this was a positive violation of court procedures.

In turn, the prosecution informed me I *might* be called as a character witness!

"What?" I exclaimed in absolute astonishment.

"Why not? You worked several years for Mr. Parkinson Jr. In that time, you had abuse from Percival Parkinson. You were unreasonably accused of a crime that was eventually proved you did not commit. More recently, you were hired by Parkinson's late accountant and have assisted the police in their enquiries."

"Yes, but don't you think my testimony would be seen as loaded in favor of the prosecution?"

"No, not at all."

On my return to the office, there was a message on my answering machine.

* * *

Mario was back in France for the last time. Having disposed of almost everything other than a few remaining items being held by the auction house; he was now concentrating on the Faberge egg.

The portrait of a 'Young Man' had already been returned to its rightful owners in Poland. In view of the fact that the owners were receiving a gift worth several millions, the parcel was sent DHL, with tracking, delivery payment *due on arrival.*

Mario had decided to 'fence' the Faberge egg and forward the proceeds to the *World Jewish Congress* with any future funds. He had been assured that disposing of such an item would not present a problem.

He had now transferred a total of 63,000,000 GB pounds from his holding bank, accompanied by a confirmation letter on his own bank letterhead, each about one month apart to avoid prying eyes. He now held a 'carry-over' of three million pounds sterling. This, added to the funds from the sale of the *Senator Explorer* and his share of the proceeds from the wreck, would be sufficient to keep him solvent until his next venture.

The following morning, Mario concluded his business in France. Before returning to England, he made a final visit to his bank in Liechtenstein.

On his return to England, Mario told Eddy, Nick, Collin and Ian he would be away for a couple months and would contact them sometime after he returned, as he might be in need of their services once again. While away, Mario would have plenty of time to bring his next plan up to fulfillment!

*   *   *

I was relieved to be told I would not be called as a witness in the Percival Parkinson case. I was much relieved, as I did not want to be put to the temptation of losing my cool.

The powers that be decided there was sufficient evidence to convict Percival—without anything from me.

Christina and I did not go to the last days of the trial. We would know the result soon enough, and I was back in busy mode with an additional two new clients, both of whom had paid retainers up front.

Percival was found guilty of embezzlement, as well as fraud. Sentencing would be in four days' time; this would allow the court time to get references and investigate any past activities, the results of which would determine the severity of his sentence. It was possible Percival might be recalled to answer charges of conspiracy to murder. It was also possible Parkinson Jr. could be out of prison before Percival.

Regrettably, there was, so far, not enough evidence to bring charges against Percival regarding the death of Walter Prendigast. The case was still ongoing, and it was considered the truth may never be known. Only time would tell.

AUTHOR'S NOTE

S OME READERS MAY NOTICE THE odd fact that some entries in this novel may appear to be in error. There *are* errors in this book and even with the finest research and researchers in the world, mistakes will occur. Research for me is now difficult, so I have to rely on the Internet and other informative media. My hope is that readers will remember this novel is a work of fiction—although certain true events *have* been interwoven.

Printed in the United States
By Bookmasters